Now that I had tuned back into the present, I realized that I was hungry. Stiff, too, after sitting in almost the same position for two solid hours. Still clutching the diary, I stood up, taking care not to smash my head on the beams.

As I did, a piece of paper slid out from the pages of the book. I picked it up and began to unfold it. I tried to be extra careful, since it was as crumbly as the pages of the photograph album.

I held it up to the light, trying to make out what was written on it. It was written in still another handwriting. And from what I could see, it looked like a poem.

"What on earth . . . ?" I leaned over closer to the window, where the light was better. Finally, I was able to read it.

"Find the treasure" was written on top. My heart was racing as I read the poem underneath. . . .

BURIED TREASURE . . . IN MY OWN ATTIC?

Cynthia Blair

FAWCETT JUNIPER • NEW YORK

RLI: $\dfrac{\text{VL 4 \& up}}{\text{IL 5 \& up}}$

A Fawcett Juniper Book
Published by Ballantine Books
Copyright © 1994 by Cynthia Blair

All rights reserved under International and Pan-American Copyright Conventions. Published in the United States of America by Ballantine Books, a division of Random House, Inc., New York, and simultaneously in Canada by Random House of Canada Limited, Toronto.

Library of Congress Catalog Card Number: 93-90878

ISBN 0-449-70427-0

Manufactured in the United States of America

First Edition: May 1994

10 9 8 7 6 5 4 3 2 1

chapter
one

"Carla Far-rell! Carla Far-rell! Body shaped like a cracker barrel!"

It happened while I was walking home from school, lugging a stack of books, minding my own business. In fact, I'd been feeling pretty good as I bopped along to my favorite radio station, pounding through my Walkman straight into my ears. The music was loud, just the way I like it. Still, it wasn't too loud to keep me from hearing somebody yell out the open window of a passing car.

I turned without thinking. Sure enough; there was Skip Jones, his head hanging out the back window as the car whizzed by. He was sticking out his tongue and rolling his eyes, making a face that was even uglier than his real one.

It all happened so fast. Before I knew it, the car turned the corner and vanished. The moment had passed. But I was left feeling like a balloon that had just lost a wrestling match with a very sharp pin.

1

Tears stung my eyes as I shuffled away, clutching my schoolbooks tightly against my chest. They suddenly seemed much heavier than before. And as if all *that* weren't bad enough, the song I liked so much, the one that had been playing on my Walkman, ended. In its place was a commercial. Something about a pimple cream.

I rounded the corner of Greenlawn and Cedar, where an old abandoned building made of crumbling gray brick has been sitting on a lot covered with overgrown weeds for as long as I can remember. I've always thought of it as the biggest eyesore in all of Hanover.

I thought that my being there at that particular moment was very symbolic.

Not that this was the first time I'd starred in a scene like this. Ever since I was little, I've been the kid that all the others picked on. The unpopular one. The one who got treated like I had the plague—a particularly contagious strain. You see, in that great theatrical production known as Life, I have always played the role of the Fat Girl.

That's right; I'm the one who got called names like Fatso and Thunder Thighs and Brontosaurus Butt. I was the last to be chosen for a team in gym class—and whoever got stuck with me always let out a loud groan. Instead of the cool outfits all the other girls wore, I had to wear baggy, stretchy clothes, whatever I could manage to fit over my round middle, my round arms, and whatever other round parts of me needed covering up. And the day the school nurse weighed everybody—calling out the dreaded numbers in front of the whole class—was the worst day of every year.

The rest of me isn't too bad looking, I suppose. My hair is your basic short, dark, curly variety, and my eyes are an ordinary shade of brown. Pretty standard looks for a twelve-year-old. Except, of course, from the neck down. That's where all my problems have always come in. And that's what cast me into the role of outsider—not exactly a piece of cake, if you'll excuse the expression.

I let out a long sigh. My Walkman picked that moment to shoot a loud blast of static into my ear. Then: "Help, Unlimited is looking for volunteers. If you're a teen with extra time, a teen who'd like to help make our world a better place . . ."

The singsong voice of the woman on the radio commercial sounded like fingernails being dragged across a blackboard. I switched my Walkman off. I wished I could switch off my bad mood as easily. But since I couldn't, I decided to go for the next best thing. I backtracked a few steps to change my route, heading off Greenlawn and onto a residential side street.

As I did, I made a point of reminding myself that lately, there wasn't only bad news in my life. There was good news, too. The days of being a total social outcast were over. No more lonely afternoons with nothing better to do after I finished my homework than watch reruns on TV. No more endless weekends alone, with nobody to hang out with. For the first time in my life, I felt like an *insider*. That was because I'd just made two of the best friends of my entire life, Samantha Langtree and Betsy Crane.

A couple of months earlier, all three of us had started seventh grade at a brand-new school. Through some magical process—or, to be honest, a special project in our English class—we found one another. We became even more than friends; we became the Bubble Gum Gang. The way all that came about is kind of a long story, one I'll save for later.

What I *will* say now is that a lot of things have changed since the three of us teamed up. One major change was that I decided to go on a diet. A *real* diet. Oh, sure, I'd tried them before. In fact, that past summer, my parents had sent me to a special camp for overweight girls. It was supposed to be my big chance to take off all those extra pounds that even my grandmother no longer referred to as "baby fat." Unfortunately, instead of learning how to eat sensibly, I'd ended up learning how to smuggle mail-order gourmet chocolate-chip cookies into Camp Breezy Pines. The extra pounds remained.

It wasn't until I went back to school in the fall and became involved with the Drama Club that I realized my lifelong habit of overeating was hurting nobody but myself. Once that fact hit me over the head like a frozen foot-long hot dog, it was easy making the decision to start eating like a twelve-year-old girl instead of a football team that had been stranded on a desert island without a crumb for six whole months. I'd lost weight, too. For a while. Then I'd leveled off. That was a little bit discouraging. Well, maybe a whole lot discouraging.

Still, no matter how uncooperative the scale had been during the past week or so, I recognized that I never could have gotten even this far without the support of the other members of the Bubble Gum Gang. And at that moment, finding them was the only thing I wanted to do.

I knew they were over at Sam's house. I would have been there myself if I hadn't stayed after school for some extra help in math. Actually, I'd had every intention of putting my social life on hold that afternoon, at least long enough to do some heavy-duty cramming for the math test that Ms. Ellsworth had scheduled for the next day. But algebra could wait. A life crisis couldn't.

Samantha Langtree lives in the biggest, grandest, most impressive house in all of Hanover. I guess I could even call it a mansion without being accused of exaggerating. Every time I walk across her front lawn—about as big as the campgrounds at a national park—I find myself pretending I'm going to a ball at my local neighborhood palace. It's that fancy. White columns, huge windows hung with flowing drapes, the whole bit. On that particular November day, there were rows and rows of colorful, perfect chrysanthemums running along the front of the house, even though by that point autumn was getting to be old news.

A lot of people have always assumed that because Samantha is the middle daughter in the town's wealthiest family, she must be a snob. Boy, are they ever wrong. Sam is the sweetest, nicest, kindest person I've ever met ... with the possible exception of Betsy, my *other* best friend. Still, she'd had a rough time. Because people assumed a rich girl like her was a snob, they ended up acting like snobs themselves, treating her as an outcast. The result was that she and I really did have a lot in common.

As I knocked on the door, I took a moment to breathe in the crisp fall air. I noticed then how hungry I was. Suddenly, I was dying for something autumnal, some food that was perfect for November. Hot apple pie, maybe, right out of the oven. Or nutty apple crisp that smelled like cinnamon and nutmeg. Skip Jones's cruel words were still ringing in my ears, and I longed for something sweet to make me feel better, at least for a little while. I let out another long sigh. With Samantha and Betsy behind my diet a thousand percent, I had a feeling a plain old apple was more along the lines of what my after-school snack would turn out to be.

Sometimes I think we members of the Bubble Gum Gang are so much in tune that we can read one another's minds. As Betsy threw open the front door, she was munching on—you guessed it—an apple.

"Carla!" she cried. Then her smile faded. She pushed aside a strand of fiery red hair that had fallen into her green eyes and frowned. "Wait a minute. I thought you were going to dedicate the rest of today to mastering algebra."

I appreciated her concern. Especially since panicking over a math test is something that Betsy Crane would be bound to have a hard time understanding. To call her bright would be an understatement. Betsy's always been the smartest kid in the entire school. But instead of being respected for her superior brain, she, too, spent most of her life as an outsider. Just as I had been called the fat girl and Samantha the snob, Betsy had long been labeled "teacher's pet." Not exactly the road to popularity.

That is, until Samantha and I came along. We recognized that Betsy had no desire to act superior, not to us or to anyone else. What her braininess did, in fact, was make her an expert at solving mysteries, something that had already come in handy during the Bubble Gum Gang's various escapades.

But at that moment, I was in no mood for reminiscing about our past glories.

"It would take me more like twenty years to master algebra," I muttered to Betsy, stepping inside. "You're right, though. I was going to throw myself into it this afternoon. At least, that was my plan before Skip Jones yelled an insult at me out the car window as he rode by."

"Skip Jones?" Samantha repeated, coming out of the kitchen and toward the front hallway. As usual, she looked like she'd just stepped out of the pages of a magazine. It's not only her long, silky blond hair or her big blue eyes, either. She also happens to dress like a model, since she buys a lot of her clothes in places like Paris and London and Milan, Italy. Not exactly the local mall.

She, too, was munching on an apple. Another healthy eater. That's the Bubble Gum Gang for you. We all stick together like . . . well, like bubble gum.

"What did that airhead say?" she demanded. Already her protective streak was coming out.

My eyes were glued to the floor as I repeated the hateful little poem Skip Jones had screeched at me. I was trying to stay calm, but it was all I could do to keep from crying. When I finally looked up and saw the sympathetic looks on Betsy's and Samantha's faces, it took everything I had to hold those tears back in my eyeballs, where they belonged.

"That jerk!" Betsy cried. "What's the matter with that boy?"

"He's hardly one to talk!" Samantha exclaimed. "I don't think Skip Jones could find his way out of a plastic bag."

"Thanks, you two." I tried to smile. I ended up doing a pretty bad job. In fact, I burst into tears.

"Why are people so mean?" I sobbed, plopping my books and my Walkman onto the nearest chair so I could use my hands to cover my face. "Why can't they just leave me alone?"

"Skip Jones is an idiot," Betsy insisted. "And I wish he were here right now so I could tell him exactly what I think of him."

"Betsy's right," Samantha added soothingly, patting my shoulder. "Skip *is* an idiot. Not only that; he's mean, too. But not everybody is mean."

Betsy was nodding. "*We* like you just the way you are."

By that point, I had managed to control my sobs so that they were only little gasping sounds. I allowed Sam and Betsy to lead me into the kitchen, where the three of us sat down. There was a big wooden bowl of apples in the middle of the table. I looked at them as if they were my worst enemies.

"I—I'm sorry about this," I said. Samantha handed me a tissue, and I did my best to mop up the remains of the flood on my face. "I guess I've been feeling kind of blue lately."

Samantha nodded. "So we see."

"I bet you're feeling let down because the school

play ended," Betsy added. "You put so much time and energy into the Drama Club, Carla. It stands to reason that now that the fall production is over, you're bound to be left feeling at loose ends."

I hadn't thought of that. It was true that for the past few weeks, the school's production of *Our Town*, the play by Thornton Wilder, had been occupying almost every second of my existence. I breathed, slept, and even ate that play. Being in it turned out to be one of the highlights of my entire life. So I realized that Betsy was probably right when she suggested that having that chapter of my life end would no doubt have an effect.

On top of that, of course, was the business about the way I'd suddenly stopped losing weight. Sure, I was still eating healthy foods, living on snacks of carrots and pretzels . . . and apples. I took walks every chance I got. Long ones, all around Hanover. Or, on rainy days, all around the Hanover Mall. For a while, the payoff had been terrific. The pounds had just fallen off.

This is a breeze, I'd thought, wondering why it had taken me so long to figure out this was all it took to get rid of all that miserable, unwanted flesh.

But then, suddenly, it got harder. I'd "plateau'd," as they say. That means I'd reached a certain weight at which my body said, "Okay. That's good enough." The fat cells wouldn't budge, and neither would the scale. It was discouraging to be working so hard, eating right and exercising, while the scale thumbed its nose at me day after day. I'd tried not to think about it too much, but the fact remained that having stopped losing weight was getting me down, too.

All in all, I had a whole list of perfectly good reasons for bursting into tears. For feeling just generally crummy, too. And Samantha and Betsy, being the sensitive souls they both are, could easily see what a hard time I was having.

"Oh, Carla, is there anything we can do to help?" Betsy sounded so desperate that I found myself wishing I could help *her*.

"I have an idea," Samantha piped up. "What do you say we go rent a video? We can do our homework later."

"Or maybe we could go to a movie," Betsy suggested. "If we hurry, we can catch the three-thirty bus to the mall."

They looked at me expectantly, their faces lit up with hope.

"Thanks, guys," I replied. "You're both really good friends, and I truly appreciate how much you want to help."

I let out my third good, long sigh of the day. "But I'm afraid this blue mood of mine is something I'm just going to have to deal with myself."

As I said those words, I never suspected that I *would* need a little help . . . and that it would end up coming not from the Bubble Gum Gang, but from one of the most unlikely people who'd ever walked the face of the earth.

chapter
two

As I walked home, my bad mood still hovered above me like a rain cloud. Still, once again I found myself thinking about how lucky I was to be a member of the Bubble Gum Gang. Betsy, Sam, and I had given ourselves that nickname back when we first decided to band together. We had two noble purposes in mind. The first, of course, was to be good friends to one another. Each one of us was sorely in need of a couple of reliable pals. The second was to take advantage of every opportunity that came along to solve mysteries, embark on adventures, and figure out puzzles.

In fact, it had been a mystery that brought us together in the first place. Betsy first moved to Hanover a few months earlier, right before the beginning of the new school year. The apartment she moved into with her mother and her brother happened to be next door to a tumbledown old house. The house was haunted—at least, that was its reputation. And from the start Betsy was convinced that the rumor was true. She decided to investigate. In the end, she not only discovered the real story behind the haunting; she also discovered Sam and me.

That was just the beginning. We'd known each other for only a couple of months so far, yet we already had an impressive list of sleuthing successes to our credit. There was a case involving shoplifting at the mall, one based on sneaky doings at Samantha's father's company, a third investigating repeated incidents of vandalism in our very own school . . . nothing was too tough for our fearless trio.

As for the name, that was Betsy's idea. She's a big fan of bubble gum. In fact, she chews it whenever she's nervous. And when you're in the mystery-solving business, being nervous is part of the game. So calling ourselves "the Bubble Gum Gang" was a natural. We tried the name out and—here goes one of my favorite puns again—it stuck.

It was a great feeling, being part of something like that. So good, in fact, that usually just thinking about it was enough to pull me out of the worst of moods. But this was no ordinary mood. As I shuffled across the lawn of my own house, Skip Jones's meanness still had me in a funk.

Walking into the kitchen and stumbling upon my older sister didn't help.

"Oh, hi," Kelly greeted me. She glanced up from

the container of yogurt she was eating—in slow motion.

That was typical. Unlike me, Kelly has never had the slightest interest in food. It's no surprise that she's thin. She also happens to be very tall. And on top of *that*, she's also one of the prettiest girls in Hanover, with her long blond hair and big blue eyes. Real cover girl stuff. In fact, people are always saying Kelly Farrell could be a model if she wanted to. But she's only sixteen, and so she puts more time into worrying about which boy to go out with than agonizing over whether or not to launch a career plastering her face on the pages of magazines.

Since I was in one of my fat moods, I didn't feel like exchanging cheerful conversation with someone who had never known the agony of a belt that refused to be buckled. Or a cool T-shirt that looked like it was stuffed with old socks once I had put it on.

Not that it's Kelly's fault. I tried really hard not to hold her great looks against her. Oh, I'll admit that in the past we'd had our bad moments, Kelly and me. But in the end, our rocky times made the two of us closer. I actually considered her a friend. Most of the time, anyway. That particular day happened to be a major exception.

"How's school going?" she asked brightly. "You've got a big math test coming up, don't you?"

"Right," I mumbled. "Tomorrow. Well, I guess I'll go study."

I had only gotten halfway across the kitchen when she said, "Better watch out for Mom. I overheard her talking to Dad on the phone. She's in one of her clean freak moods. She's got a big project in mind . . . and it's got *your* name on it."

I knew what that meant. My mother is usually a perfectly normal person. But every few months, she gets it into her head that the main problem in our lives is that we have too much stuff cluttering them up. She picks out some area of the house—last time it was the garage—and will not rest easy until every square inch of it is spotless.

I got tired just thinking about it. It'd happened the summer before, right before I trotted off to Camp Breezy Pines. For two solid weeks I spent every waking hour sorting, dumping, polishing, reshuffling, and recycling boxes and boxes of *junk* that had been living in our garage since before Noah built the ark. I sorted nails according to size. I sorted screws according to shape. I tied up newspapers, cleaned grease off tools I couldn't even identify, carried boxes of bottles, jars, tubes, and plastic containers to the trunk of the car so they could be taken over to the recycling center.

The thought of doing something like that again made me shudder.

"Not the garage again," I whimpered. "It's still clean, isn't it?"

"It's not the garage," Kelly said seriously.

"The basement?"

"Worse." She frowned. "The attic."

"The *attic*?" Spiders. Cobwebs. Difficult decisions to make, like what exactly should be done with four ancient radios, none of which still work. "Maybe she was kidding. Maybe it's just a phase. Maybe . . ."

"Maybe this Saturday would be a good time to get started!"

My mother had just come into the kitchen, wearing a big grin. From the look on her face, I could tell she was *enjoying* the idea of her younger daughter wasting a perfectly good weekend up to her chin in other people's junk. Junk that entire tribes of spiders considered their home. That mold and mildew probably considered their vacation home. That maybe even mice . . . but that was too terrible even to think about.

"This Saturday?" I repeated, blinking. "What's the hurry?"

"You know what they say," Mom insisted. "There's no time like the present."

"Besides," Kelly volunteered cheerfully, "doing dirty work builds character."

I made a point of glaring at her.

Mom didn't notice. "Besides," she went on, "according to the weather report, this Saturday is going to be cold and rainy. That's the ideal kind of day to spend up in an attic, rummaging through old photographs and discarded clothes . . . and memories."

I would have much preferred rummaging through

the sale racks at the mall. Or hanging out with my friends. Or reading, or studying, or having my teeth cleaned . . . Suddenly, any pastime in the entire world other than weeding through dusty old cartons sounded good to me.

But I didn't exactly have a choice. That, I could tell by the gleam in Mom's eye.

"Who knows?" she said, her eyes brighter than ever. "Maybe you'll find something good up there."

"Maybe you'll find buried treasure," Kelly suggested with a smirk.

"Whoever heard of burying treasure in an attic?" I shot back. "Speaking of which, what is my dear sister Kelly's contribution to this family clean-up effort?"

She was trying to slink out the door. But Mom was too fast for her.

"Now that you mention it," my mother said thoughtfully, "I've noticed that the basement is getting out of hand. . . ."

"The *basement*!" Kelly wailed.

"Gosh, Kelly," I said, wide-eyed and innocent. "Mold, mildew, damp, dark corners . . . just think how strong *your* character's going to be!"

chapter
three

The next day, right after school, Sam and Betsy and I headed over to my house. My math test had gone okay. And I still had two full days of freedom before Saturday, Zero Hour for tackling the task of battling creepy crawlies and killer dust bunnies in an effort to clean up the attic. I should have been feeling great.

Instead, my bad mood hung on like a cold that refused to get better. As the three of us lounged around in my room—Betsy stretched out across the bed with her shoes kicked off, me in the rocking chair hugging a pillow, Sam sitting cross-legged on the floor—I was in the same old funk. Samantha and Betsy, meanwhile, were doing their best to pull me out of it.

"So, Carla," Betsy said, sounding unnaturally cheerful, "has the Drama Club made a decision yet about what play it's going to put on next?"

"It'd be great if they did a musical," Samantha

said with that same forced tone. "Then Carla could really show off her talents. She could sing, she could dance . . . and, of course, she's already proven she's a top-notch actress!"

"The Drama Club is on vacation," I mumbled. "We're not starting our next production until January. We had a meeting last week, and our adviser Ms. Hart said she feels there's too much other stuff going on, with Thanksgiving and Christmas coming up, to start anything now."

There was a long silence. I became aware of the radio, playing softly in the background. It was tuned to the same station I always listen to. None of us was really listening, which was just as well because all that was on was a bunch of commercials. I turned my attention back to my friends. I could see that their minds were clicking away.

"I'm glad to hear your math test went so well," Samantha said brightly. "That's wonderful, Carla. I knew you could do it."

"Thanks, Sam." I sighed. "Look, I know you mean well, but according to my calculations, you've already said that six times."

"Seven," Betsy corrected me. Then she, too, let out a long, loud sigh. "Look, Carla. We're not going to try to kid you. The fact is, both Sam and I are really worried about you. We've never seen you like this."

Samantha nodded. "I can count the number of times I've seen you smile in the past week on one hand."

"I'm sorry to be such a drag," I said. "It's just that, all of a sudden, it feels like there's not very much to feel good about."

Actually, that was an understatement. I didn't want to tell them how I was really feeling. Worthless. Empty. Like a failure. I was someone who couldn't lose weight. Someone who had started to crave cookies again, who was beginning to feel that the suffering involved in trying to stay trim simply wasn't worth it. Someone who mattered so little in the grand scheme of things that all I was good for was cleaning out grimy, bug-infested attics.

Still, I think they knew anyway. There was another long silence. This time, at least, a decent song was playing on the radio. Unfortunately, it happened to be one of those really depressing ones about love gone sour.

"You're not being a drag," Betsy insisted. "It's just that Sam and I have been talking about this, and . . . well, we want to help."

"Thanks, you guys. You're both great. But I don't even know what I need." A hot fudge sundae came to mind, but I pushed it right back out as fast as I could.

"Betsy and I had an idea," Samantha said gently.

"We were thinking that maybe what you need is to get involved in something outside of school."

Betsy was nodding. "Volunteering. Getting involved in an organization dedicated to helping people."

"Oh, I get it," I said. "You mean so I wouldn't have so much time to think about myself."

Betsy and Sam looked at each other. I could see the hopefulness in their eyes.

"You've got it," Samantha said.

"That's *exactly* what we were thinking," Betsy added.

I was about to protest, insisting that the last thing I needed was one more thing to do, when Sam suddenly leaned over and turned the radio up louder.

"Sh-h-h. Listen to this."

The depressing love song was over. Another commercial had taken its place.

"Help, Unlimited is looking for volunteers. If you're a teen with extra time, a teen who'd like to help make our world a better place . . ."

There it was again, that same commercial I'd heard the day before. It had come on the radio right after creepy old Skip Jones had yelled that awful rhyme out the window.

"Sam, I really don't think—"

"Wait a second." Samantha held up her hand for silence. "Betsy, give me that pencil."

The voice on the radio went on. Meanwhile Sam

jotted down the telephone number on the edge of her science notebook. By the time the commercial was over and the weather report came on, there was a look of triumph in her blue eyes.

"We've got it!" she cried. "This is it!"

I scowled. "This is *what*?"

"Exactly what you need. This is the kind of thing Betsy and I were thinking about."

"That's right," Betsy piped up. "And it sounds like they're looking for people exactly like you."

"The woman said they were looking for teenagers," I mumbled. "I'm only twelve."

"Close enough," Betsy insisted. "Besides, even if they do require volunteers to be a certain age, you can still try."

"You've got nothing to lose," said Sam. "Hey, why don't you call right now?"

"That's a great idea!" Already Betsy was handing me the phone. "I'll read off the number."

"Wait a minute!" I cried. "Aren't you forgetting one minor detail?"

Sam and Betsy looked at me, surprised.

"What?" they asked in unison.

"I don't want to do this!"

"Why don't you at least try it?" Samantha urged.

"It wouldn't hurt to call." Betsy pushed the phone a little closer to me. "The number is five-five-five . . ."

So there I was, dialing the number of Help, Unlim-

ited. I didn't particularly want to, but at the moment
it didn't seem as if I had very much choice. Not with
two eager faces watching me expectantly, hanging on
to my every word.

"Help, Unlimited!" a cheerful voice at the other
end answered. "How may I help you?"

"Uh, hello," I said after swallowing hard. "I'm
calling about the ad you've been running on the
radio. The one that says you're looking for volunteers . . ."

Little did I know that the telephone call I was being forced to make by two girls who claimed to be
my best friends was going to turn out to be one of the
most important calls I've ever made in my life.

"What am I doing here?" I asked myself as I sat
in a small waiting room, feeling like a fish out of
water.

I was surprised to find that the waiting room at
Help, Unlimited was surprisingly pleasant. It was
clean, bright, and sunny, painted a pretty shade of
blue. The walls were decorated with public service
posters, the kind that teachers are always putting up
on the bulletin boards at school. Posters reminding
people how bad smoking is for them, posters encour-
aging people to Just Say No to drugs, that kind of
thing.

There was nobody around. Not a receptionist, not
a secretary, not a single soul to take note of the fact

that I was there. It was exactly 3:30 on Friday afternoon, the time the woman on the phone—Ricky Norris—had said to come. But the place was like a ghost town.

I must admit, I was pretty nervous. Part of me felt like just taking off, forgetting the whole thing. After all, nobody had even seen me come in. But another part of me felt I owed it to my friends to follow through. I'd promised Betsy and Samantha I would do this, that I'd at least check out what this Help, Unlimited business was all about, so I didn't feel I had much choice. Still, I was beginning to think maybe I should have taken them up on their offer to come with me.

Before I had a chance to worry about it too much, a door opened and a pleasant-looking young woman in jeans poked her head out.

"Carla?" she asked, smiling. "Hi, I'm Ricky. Sorry to have kept you waiting."

I mumbled something about how it was okay because I'd just gotten there, then followed her into her office. That, too, was a bright room, with two big windows. It was painted daffodil yellow. There was a colorful rag rug on the floor that made it look positively friendly. I found myself relaxing.

Ricky sat down at her desk and picked up a clipboard. "I'm afraid that I'm going to have to ask you a million questions. But before we get started, I'm sure you have some you'd like to ask me."

"I have one," I said. "Where is everybody?"

She laughed. "I know what you're thinking—and believe me, you're hardly the first. Our organization is involved in so many different things that new people always expect our office to be a hubbub of activity. But the truth is that most of what we do is done out *there*, not in here."

She gestured toward the window, as if to indicate the rest of the world. "A few of us handle the administrative side of things—mainly, hooking up volunteers with the people who need them most. But all the actual volunteer work is done in schools, or the community rooms of churches, or even in people's homes."

I nodded to show I understood. Ricky glanced at her clipboard. "The first question I always ask applicants is, What brought you to Help, Unlimited in the first place?"

I gulped. Now *that* was a tricky question. I wasn't about to tell this nice woman that my two best friends had strong-armed me into coming in to volunteer. That they were worried about me, and this was their solution to what they saw as my problem. Frankly, admitting all that would have been kind of embarrassing.

"Well . . ." I began slowly, hunting for an answer to her question.

And then it all came pouring out. I don't know where the rush of words came from; maybe I'd been keeping it all stored up in my head without even realizing it. At any rate, when they were finally released, there was no stopping them.

"I've been feeling so blue lately," I began. "It's as if nothing in my life is going right. Somehow, I've got no real sense of purpose. No reason to get up in the morning, other than to go through the motions of the day. Oh, sure, I know I'm feeling let down because the school play I was just in is over. It was the focus of things for me for weeks. . . .

"The other thing, of course, is that I've been trying really hard to diet. At first I lost a whole bunch of weight, and I felt great about it, but now it's as if no matter how hard I try, I can't get that stupid scale to budge.

"And then there was Skip Jones. Yelling out the car window like that, calling me fat . . . That sure didn't do much to make me feel worthwhile. Anyway, some friends of mine, Samantha and Betsy, could see how crummy I've been feeling lately, and they came up with the idea that I should get involved in something that would take me outside of myself. . . ."

Suddenly I stopped. I was out of breath. I was also out of words. I realized then and there that I had gotten a little bit out of control.

Sheepishly, I said, "Sorry about that. I—I didn't mean to dump all that on you."

"Don't apologize, Carla," Ricky said softly. "I'm

glad you felt you could tell me what's really on your mind. And do you know what?"

I looked at her, blinking. "What?'

She took a deep breath, then smiled.

"I think you've come to the right place."

chapter
four

Just as the weather report had threatened, Saturday turned out to be a cold, rainy day. It was exactly the kind you'd expect from a dreary month like November. And it just so happened that I was in a pretty dreary mood as I dragged myself out of bed and shuffled downstairs to breakfast.

Kelly was sitting at the kitchen table, eating her usual breakfast of about six corn flakes. Back in the old days, breakfast used to be my favorite meal of the day. It meant waffles dripping with butter and maple syrup, stacks of pancakes so high they nearly toppled over, scrambled eggs with sausage and bacon. . . . That is, until the big diet began. Nowadays, breakfast meant bran muffins or cereal with low-fat milk.

Most mornings, I hardly missed the other stuff at all. But today was different. With the rain pounding against the windows and the long day of work stretching ahead of me, I couldn't get too excited about a bowl of cold cereal. Visions of butter and maple syrup insisted upon dancing in my head. Still, it was corn flakes that I settled for as I sat down with Kelly.

"Today's the day," she muttered, barely glancing up from her bowl. "Look out, basement, here I come."

Her mood was at the same level as mine: about twenty feet under the ground.

"Well, at least in the basement the ceilings are high enough that you'll be able to stand up," I reminded her. "*I*, meanwhile, am going to have to spend the entire day bent over like a little gnome."

"You'll be able to hear the rain on the roof." Kelly sighed. "The way our basement gets flooded, I'll probably end up standing up to my ankles in it."

"Maybe we should have a contest," I suggested. "You know, see who finds more spiders."

She cast me a dirty look.

"I was *kidding*!" I cried. "Can't you take a joke?"

Half an hour later, I was sitting cross-legged on the floor of the attic, leafing through an old photograph album. It was filled with pictures of my parents when they were young, grinning at the camera and wearing bell-bottom jeans and loud shirts in colors like orange and hot pink and Day-Glo green. To tell you the truth, those photographs were hilarious.

Maybe this won't be so bad, after all, I thought, taking a moment to glance around.

Kelly was right; it was kind of nice being up in the attic with the rain pounding down on the roof. It was only about five feet above me, so close that it sounded like the rhythmic beating of drums. There was a dim overhead light, really only a single light bulb. It was mostly the gray morning, coming in through the tiny window, that lit up the big space with the creaky wooden floors, the unfinished walls, only half covered with Sheetrock, and the exposed beams overhead. Instead of being eerie, it was actually kind of nice. Quiet. Calm. And so far, at least, I had yet to see a single spider.

All around me was—for lack of a better word—junk. Just as I'd expected, the entire attic was piled high with things that had once been important in someone's life, but now had been stuck up there and forgotten. They were packed away in cardboard cartons, for the most part. Clothes, books, toys, papers . . . who knew what else was hidden away in there? Of course, I'd be finding out soon enough. That *was* my job.

There were other things, too. An artificial Christmas tree, in three separate pieces. Four or five huge picture frames, without any pictures in them. My old dollhouse, which looked really big up here . . . and my old bicycle, which looked comically small. A few trunks were stuck way back behind all the other stuff, looking like nobody had touched them since dinosaurs roamed the earth. There was certainly a lot of stuff. And I was going to have to go through every single bit of it.

"If I'm ever going to make a dent in this," I muttered, "I'm going to have to cut short this trip down memory lane."

With a sigh, I closed the photo album. This was something I was certain my mother would want to keep—even if she did look ridiculous in those bell-bottoms. I dusted it off with one of the rags I'd brought up and put it aside. It was the first item in what was going to be the "Keep" pile.

Two hours later, the "Keep" pile was almost as high as the beams. Fortunately, the other pile, the "Throw Out" pile, was even higher.

"This is going to make Mom very happy," I said aloud, surveying my work. I must admit, I felt something very close to pride as I looked at what I'd done. Sure, I'd only attacked a quarter of the junk packed away up there. But it was a good start. And if I continued at the same rate, I might even be finished by dinnertime.

I was thinking about taking a break, climbing down the rickety ladder connecting the trap door of the attic with the rest of the house, when I noticed another pile of photo albums. This stack looked as if it were about to come tumbling down. I had just moved a bunch of cartons; that had probably set them off balance, I reasoned. Besides, photo albums were easy. All I had to do was dust them off and stick them in the "Keep" pile. Eventually, I would find a carton big enough to stash away the whole kit and kaboodle for *another* couple of decades.

"I'll just move these out of the way, and then I'll head downstairs," I mumbled.

Actually, I was curious to see if my legs still worked. I'd been sitting in practically the same cross-legged position since nine o'clock that morning, and I had serious doubts about whether or not they, too, were at this point only as useful as the collection of broken radios encircling the "Throw Out" pile.

I leaned over and grabbed the stack of photograph albums. As I did, I caught sight of a metal plaque on the trunk they'd been sitting on. In the dim light of the attic, I could make out the letters, "C.A.F."

"Hey!" I cried. "Those are *my* initials!"

My full name is Carla Anne Farrell. That's right, C.A.F. Yet I had never in my life owned a trunk . . . especially one like this.

I leaned forward to get a better look. In the dim light of the attic, I could see that this one was so old that it could have been a prop in a movie. It was made out of black metal, a heavy, solid thing that looked as if it could easily have withstood a trip across the Atlantic Ocean . . . or a trip to the moon. The dust on it was almost as thick as moon dust, too. It was huge, the kind that magicians regularly stuff smiling assistants into.

I was fascinated. It wasn't only the odd-looking

trunk, either; it was also the initials. C.A.F. My initials . . . but not my trunk.

Who had stolen my initials?

That old saying, the one about there being only one way to find out, immediately popped into my mind. And so I brushed aside enough dust to get a good look at the clasp, struggled to unfasten it, and opened up the trunk.

The lid creaked so loudly that I jumped. I half expected a skeleton to jump out. But there was no skeleton, just more dust.

"Gee," I muttered. "Maybe dinosaurs really were the last ones who used this trunk."

Normally, picturing dinosaurs storing their winter coats and boots in a trunk would have made me laugh. But I was in no mood for laughing. I was too busy trying to unravel the mystery of the dust-covered trunk . . . one that, once upon a time, had belonged to C.A.F.—whoever that was.

I leaned over so I could get a better look. It wasn't easy, in that light. I could see dark, shadowy shapes . . . but I couldn't tell what they were. Slowly I stuck my hand in, afraid of what my exploring fingers might encounter. I just hoped this wasn't where all the spiders were hiding.

But what my fingers met up with wasn't a spider. Or even a spiderweb. In fact, it was the softest fabric I had ever felt in my life.

I grabbed hold of it and pulled it out. It turned out

to be a long dress, a beautiful shade of purple, made of velvet and decorated with lace. It was so old-fashioned that it looked like a costume in a play.

"Look at this!" I cried, holding it up against me. "Oooh, I wonder if it'll fit!"

Then I thought of something: if there was *one* great dress in that trunk, chances were good that there was another . . . and another. Eagerly I reached back in. Sure enough, before long I'd unpacked a whole wardrobe of wonderful, old-fashioned dresses.

Some of them were thick, heavy woolens in dark colors. Others were flowery cottons, trimmed with ruffles, ribbons, and bows. One was made entirely of cream-colored lace. It was easily the most beautiful of all. They were all different, but there was one thing they definitely had in common. They all belonged to another time, an era that was long, long ago.

Then I noticed something else about the dresses. They were all incredibly *narrow*.

"No way I'd ever fit in these," I grumbled, putting them aside.

I reached back into the trunk. So far, I'd hardly made a dent in all the stuff packed away in there. So I kept going. This was turning out to be as much fun as opening presents on Christmas morning. And I was anything but disappointed. What wonderful things there were inside that trunk! I found big, floppy straw hats, their brims edged with ribbons and silk flowers. Incredible shoes, nothing at all like the bulky Reeboks I was wearing. There was also a mirror and a hairbrush, as well as some jewelry. The jewelry didn't look like it was particularly valuable, but I still had fun looking through the pins and earrings and strings of beads. Those, at least, I could wear.

I was having a blast, but I still had no idea who C.A.F. was.

I had just made up my mind that the only way I'd solve this mystery was to ask my mom when I knelt beside the trunk for what I expected to be one last time. I wanted to check to make sure I'd gotten everything out so I could begin putting it all back *in*.

Instead, as my groping hand checked the bottom of the trunk, I let out a loud gasp.

The trunk wasn't empty at all. In fact, I had just stumbled upon the *real* treasure.

Slowly, carefully, I lifted out the things I'd found stashed at the bottom of the trunk. A photograph album, so old that the paper pages crumbled in my hand . . . and a diary.

My heart was pounding. Maybe I was finally going to find out who C.A.F. was, the woman who owned all those beautiful dresses and floppy old-fashioned hats and weird shoes. I held my breath as I opened the diary, appreciating the fact that I was about to pry into someone's innermost thoughts.

I didn't get very far before I let out another loud

gasp. In fact, I'd only gotten as far as the first page. The very first words in the whole diary caught me so off guard that I nearly dropped it.

"June 21," someone had written in a neat, round handwriting. And, right after, the year "1912."

Nineteen-twelve! That was almost a whole century ago! The diary I was holding in my hands was a real antique. I, meanwhile, was more curious than ever to find out more about the person who'd written it. I leaned over more closely so that I could make out the words, even in the dim light of a dark old attic on a rainy afternoon.

"Dear Diary," it began. "Today is my twelfth birthday. Mother gave me this diary, so it seems fitting that I end the day by writing my very first entry. It was a wonderful birthday. We had a wonderful tea party on the lawn, with fresh strawberry ice cream and lemonade. Father got the other members of his barbershop quartet to sing 'Happy Birthday.' I wore the most wonderful dress I've ever owned, made of cream-colored lace. I also put on my straw hat with the yellow silk flowers. I felt very grown-up."

By this point, my heart was really pounding. I could hardly wait to read on. I felt as if I had just stumbled upon a brand-new friend, someone who was exactly my age but had lived in another time entirely. What a different world it was, too! Barbershop quartets, homemade ice cream, birthday dresses made of lace. . . .

But who was she? I still had no idea who C.A.F.
was. I flipped through the diary, hoping to find out.
Nothing. I was just about to give up when I had a
brainstorm. I turned to the inside front cover of the
book. Sure enough, my hunch was right. In a totally
different handwriting was written the words, "Happy
Birthday to my Dear Daughter Charlotte. Love,
Mother." The date that was written up above was the
same.

Charlotte. At last I was getting somewhere. My
new friend's name was Charlotte. And with the last
initial being "F," I suspected Charlotte's last name
was Farrell.

Slowly another brainstorm was forming in my
mind. I did some quick calculations, counting off decades on my fingers, and came up with a new theory.

C.A.F., Charlotte Farrell, was probably my great-
grandfather's sister.

"Could it be?" I wondered aloud. I opened the
photo album to the first page. There, smiling back at
me, was a black-and-white photograph of a girl about
my age, smiling shyly at the camera. The name
handwritten underneath was "Charlotte Annabelle
Farrell." I looked at the picture more closely. Even in
the pale light, I could see that Charlotte looked just
like me.

Eagerly I turned back to my reading. Within seconds the attic ceased to exist. Gone was the bleak

November day. Instead, I was transported back in time.

Page after page took me on a walk side by side with Charlotte. After I'd relived every moment of her birthday party, I learned all about how she'd spent her summer, right here in Hanover. But back then it was an entirely different place. There was a swimming hole somewhere nearby, where she spent long lazy afternoons frolicking with her brothers and sisters and cousins. There were big church picnics and traveling carnivals and Sunday school pageants. When I read that she'd had the lead role in the last pageant—and, as she proudly reported, gotten more applause than anyone else—I burst out laughing.

"Charlotte," I said aloud, "you're just like me!"

When I finally came out of my trance and glanced at my watch, I was amazed to see that it was almost one o'clock. Two hours had passed! I'd been so lost in Charlotte's world that I'd forgotten all about lunch. And that, I must admit, was a first for me.

Now that I had tuned back into the present, I realized that I was hungry. Stiff, too, after sitting in almost the same position for two solid hours. Still clutching the diary, I stood up, taking care not to smash my head on the beams.

As I did, a piece of paper slid out from the pages of the book. I picked it up and began to unfold it. I tried to be extra careful, since it was as crumbly as the pages of the photograph album.

I held it up to the light, trying to make out what was written on it. It was written in still another handwriting, different from both Charlotte's and her mother's. And from what I could see, it looked like a poem.

"What on earth . . . ?" I leaned closer to the window, where the light was better. Finally, I was able to read it.

"Find the treasure," was written on top. My heart was racing as I read the poem underneath.

To find what matters more to me
Than anything on earth,
To see the treasure I most love,
The one with greatest worth,

Go where voices sing a gentle song,
Where faces lift toward heaven,
Where sunlight streams through colored glass.
Behind, at number seven,

There, upon the grass so green,
Are stones that last and last.
Find the oldest on the hill.
Face east, and travel past

To the valley down below.
And there, with careful measure
Walk small steps. Count twenty-nine,
And there you'll find the treasure.

"A treasure map!" I squealed. "A real, genuine, authentic treasure map!"

"Talking to yourself?"

I jumped at the sound of someone else's voice. I blinked a few times, trying to get my bearings. Then I saw it was only Kelly, poking her head up through the trap door.

"Uh, no, I just, uh . . ." Instinctively I stuck the treasure map behind my back. "I just found, uh, an old art project of mine from kindergarten."

"Fascinating." Kelly let out a yawn. "How's it going up here? Find anything else interesting?"

"Uh, no. Nothing at all. Just the usual junk, the kind of stuff you'd expect to find stuck up in an attic somewhere."

"Well, if it makes you feel any better, slaving away in the basement hasn't been much better. But it's time for lunch. In honor of our family cleanup, Dad and Mom offered to take us out for burgers and shakes. Want to come?"

Shakes? That sounded promising. But before I could stop myself, I said, "Make mine a diet cola and you're on. Just give me five minutes. I'll be right down."

"Don't forget to brush the cobwebs out of your hair," Kelly said as she started down the ladder.

"Huh?" I reached up and began patting my head.

"Only kidding," she called.

Carefully I packed all the clothes back into the

trunk. I slipped the "find the treasure" poem inside the pages of the diary, then put those back, too, along with the photograph album. I closed the trunk and draped an old blanket over it.

" 'Bye for now, Charlotte," I whispered before I started down the ladder. "I'm going out now ... but don't worry. I'll be back soon."

chapter
five

"That was awesome," Betsy exclaimed, picking the chocolate sprinkles off her raspberry frozen yogurt with a pink plastic spoon. "I loved that movie."

"I was so scared at the end that I couldn't watch," said Samantha. "I kept my hands over my eyes for the last fifteen minutes."

Betsy laughed. "I saw you peeking!"

"How about you?" Samantha asked me. "What'd you think of the movie, Carla?"

I shrugged. "Pretty good, I guess." I spooned some chocolate frozen yogurt into my mouth, without bothering to taste it. "To tell you the truth, I had trouble keeping my mind on the movie."

Both Samantha and Betsy burst out laughing.

"So we noticed!" Betsy cried. "As a matter of fact, it looks like you're still out there in dreamland!"

"What do you mean?" I asked, surprised.

"I think what Betsy means," Samantha said calmly,

43

"is that for the past five minutes, you've been eating *my* frozen yogurt. And you *hate* blueberry!"

I looked down. Sure enough, I'd eaten a good portion of Samantha's frozen yogurt. Meanwhile, my cup of chocolate was pushed off to the side, back behind one of the paper napkin dispensers that are on every table at YoYo's Yogurt. And Samantha was right; I did hate blueberry. I could feel my face turning as pink as the raspberry yogurt Betsy was happily eating away.

"Sorry," I mumbled. "I guess I am kind of distracted tonight."

Now that my friends had caught me with my head in the clouds, I had to admit I'd known it all along, even though I'd thought I was doing a good job of covering it up. All that Saturday evening, even as I'd sat through what was supposed to be the scariest movie of the year, I'd been totally preoccupied with Charlotte—and the mysterious poem that was actually a treasure map. I'd memorized it by that point, and I kept repeating the first lines over and over in my head. Clearly they referred to a church . . . but which church? I was dying to find out, but it would simply have to wait.

"Since I ate most of your yogurt, Samantha, the least I can do is go get you another."

"That's okay. Just give me part of your chocolate."

Once all that had been settled, Betsy and Sam looked at me expectantly.

"Okay, Carla," Samantha said, folding her hands on the table. "What is it that's got you so preoccupied that you can't even forget it on a Saturday night?"

"I bet I know." Betsy grinned. "It's Help, Unlimited, right? We never did give you a chance to tell us how your interview went yesterday."

"Were you accepted?" Sam asked eagerly.

"What did they ask you?" Betsy chimed in.

"Hold on!" I insisted, laughing. "Give me a chance! The interview went fine. This really nice woman, Ricky Norris, asked me every question you could possibly imagine. What my hobbies are, what my favorite subjects are at school, whether I'd prefer working with adults or kids, all kinds of stuff.

"As for being accepted, I don't know yet. I am kind of young, Ricky said, and she had to clear it with some other people in the organization. She's calling me on Monday to let me know." I stuck some frozen yogurt—chocolate, this time—into my mouth. "There. Any more questions?"

"You must be very excited," said Betsy. "I bet you can't wait to find out what your assignment's going to be."

"Actually, there's something even more exciting that's happened to me since then," I told them. "I spent the entire day cleaning out the attic, which I expected to be torture. Instead, I found the most incredible thing. . . ."

"I wonder if Carla's going to work with children," Samantha said. "When the woman at Help, Unlimited asked if you preferred working with adults or children, what did you say?"

"Children," I answered impatiently. "Look, aren't you even the least bit interested in hearing about a treasure map?"

"A *what*?" Betsy and Samantha cried in unison.

"You heard me correctly. A treasure map. Actually, it's a poem, but it's full of clues that lead to buried treasure."

"Hold on a minute," said Betsy, holding up her hands. "I think you'd better go back to the beginning."

So I did. First I took a deep breath. Then I told them all about the dusty old trunk I'd found in the back corner of the attic, half hidden under the stack of photo albums. I told them all about C.A.F., the sister of my great-grandfather, Charlotte Annabelle Farrell, who back in 1912 was a twelve-year-old girl, just like me. I went on to tell them about the photograph of her I'd found, as well as the wonderful diary . . . and of course the treasure map.

"A treasure map?" Samantha repeated. She was acting as if she didn't quite believe all this.

"That's right. And from what I could tell, the treasure was hidden right here in Hanover. Of course, it *was* quite a while ago. . . ."

"Slightly more than eighty years, to be exact!" Betsy exclaimed. "Carla, you don't really think there's still a treasure buried somewhere in Hanover, do you?"

"If there ever was, in the first place," Samantha added.

I was astonished. "What's going on here? Where's your sense of adventure? What about the Bubble Gum Gang's commitment to unraveling mysteries? Seeking adventure? Solving puzzles?"

"Thanks, but I'll stick to mysteries that take place in my own time, not almost a century ago." Betsy looked annoyed. "Carla, I think it's great that you're getting to know your ancestor through her diaries and all that. But wouldn't you rather be putting your energy into something from the here and now . . . something like your volunteer work for Help, Unlimited?"

"But . . . but this could be the most exciting thing that's every happened to me!" I insisted.

Betsy and Samantha merely cast each other skeptical looks.

I couldn't believe what I was seeing. Was it really possible that the other members of the Bubble Gum Gang were more excited about some silly old volunteer organization than searching for buried treasure?

"Well . . . let's see the diary," Betsy finally suggested. I got the feeling she was only pretending to be interested.

I could feel my cheeks turning pink. "I, uh, don't have it here."

"We'll come over tomorrow to take a look," said Samantha.

"Well, uh, I . . ."

It was funny. Now that I actually had a chance to share my great-grandaunt's diary with other people, I was realizing just how special it was to me. It was so special, in fact, that I felt protective of it, as if I wanted to be very careful about whom I showed it to. And even though Sam and Betsy were such good friends, their inability to get as excited about it as I was—in fact, to consider something like joining some volunteer group more important—made me reluctant to tell them anything more about it.

"If you don't mind," I said softly, "they're kind of private. I, uh, I'm not ready to show them to anybody yet."

Sam and Betsy looked startled. But they both shrugged.

"Okay, Carla, whatever you say," said Betsy.

I felt bad . . . at least a little. But somehow, I couldn't help feeling that Charlotte Annabelle Farrell would have wanted it this way.

It wasn't until I was rushing off to my very first volunteering session that I was actually able to muster up some enthusiasm for the whole idea. It was Tuesday, right after school, and I was rushing to catch the 3:15 bus across town. True to her word, Ricky Norris had called me after school on Monday.

"Congratulations!" she'd bubbled. "Not only do we want you to join our team, we also have your first assignment all lined up."

"Oh, boy," I breathed.

I meant that as an expression of dismay. Fortunately, Ricky misunderstood.

"I knew you'd be excited," she said. "Let me fill you in on the details."

A million different possibilities raced through my mind. What was my noble mission going to be? Teaching grateful immigrants how to speak English? Visiting a home for senior citizens and reading to them? Maybe going to see sick children in a hospital, doing puppet shows and cheering up their otherwise boring day?

"You're going to be working with a third-grade girl named Annie Cooper."

"Just one girl?" I blurted out.

"Yes, that's right. It's kind of like the Big Brother and Big Sister programs. The idea is that the volunteer works one-on-one with someone who's going through a troubled period."

Great, just great, I thought. There go all my visions of lighting up the lives of dozens of thankful souls.

Somehow, the idea of helping just one person sounded much more difficult, as well as less rewarding. It was kind of like the difference between putting on a play onstage in front of hundreds of people and reciting a poem for one lone listener.

Then something else occurred to me. "A troubled period?" I repeated. "What do you mean, troubled?"

"Actually, I'm not sure. I've never actually met Annie. But according to her file . . ." Ricky's voice trailed off, and she was quiet for a few seconds. I knew she was reading somebody else's notes about Annie Cooper, trying to sum her up in a few short words. I, meanwhile, was holding my breath.

"I can't find anything specific here," Ricky finally reported. "It just says that she's having a hard time in school. Her grades are terrible; she doesn't have any friends. . . ."

"I can relate to that!"

I was beginning to think that maybe this wouldn't be so bad, after all. From the looks of things, this Annie person and I already had something in common.

The idea of becoming Annie Cooper's best friend, becoming the bright light shining through someone else's fog, was appealing. And that was exactly what I was thinking about as I plopped down in a seat on the bus, headed way across town, toward Millard Fillmore Elementary School.

I already had everything worked out. From the start, Annie and I were going to hit it off. This poor, lonely girl would be so grateful that somebody was finally taking an interest in her that she would rush to my side. She'd probably want to hold my hand, I decided, since she'd instantly see me as a big sister. A kind, helpful, wonderful big sister.

And the fun we would have! I could hardly wait to start taking Annie around town. I would show her some of the things I loved, share some of my favorite pastimes with her. We'd go to the movies. We'd go to the museum, and I'd read her every one of the plaques. We'd do art projects, bake cookies together . . . maybe I'd even take her to the theater.

I was just launching Annie Cooper on a tremendous career as a world-famous actress—one in which she was *almost* as famous as I was—when the bus pulled up in front of her elementary school. I had to put the fantasy on hold, for now. But I didn't mind. After all, it was time for me to meet the girl whose life I was about to change.

That was what was running through my mind. And so I was really caught off guard when I strode confidently into the school library, where we were scheduled to meet, and the moment I walked through the door, a book came flying across the room at me.

"Ow!" I cried, grabbing my leg. It was only a paperback, but even so, when it smacked me on the knee, it hurt.

The pain was only part of it. I was also surprised. Where had that book come from? Had it fallen off a shelf? Or was it possible that somebody had actually thrown it at me?

I turned in the direction from which the book had come. Standing there with her arms folded across her chest, wearing a mean expression, was an eight-year-old girl.

"I know who you are," she accused. "And I already don't like you. Why don't you just go home?"

I forgot all about my throbbing knee. Instead, I just stared. The girl was dressed in red corduroy pants with a big rip in them and a blue and green striped shirt. Not only was the shirt too big, it also had a big black stain on it. Her brown hair was kind of messy. It was pulled back into a ponytail, but some of it was falling out of the elastic band.

She had freckles across her nose, and big, dark brown eyes. She might have been cute. It was hard to tell, since the look on her face was so nasty that she made Skip Jones look like Santa Claus.

"Are . . . are you Annie?" I croaked.

"What about it?" she shot back.

I still didn't quite get it. "I'm Carla. I was sent here by Help, Unlimited to—"

"Yeah, I know who you are. You're some goody-goody high school girl who wants to be my pal, right? Well, thanks, but no thanks. I don't need any pals."

I was stunned. I looked around the library, wondering if there was anybody around to help me out. From what I could see, there wasn't a soul in sight.

"Is the school librarian around?" I asked, trying to sound cheerful.

"Nah. She goes home as soon as the bell rings."

Annie shrugged. "It's just as well. I mean, it's not as if she likes kids or anything."

"Of course she likes children!" I protested. "Otherwise, why would she be a librarian in an elementary school?"

"Maybe she hates kids so much that she wants a chance to drive them crazy. After all, that's all she does. Day after day, all she does is bug us."

I found myself glancing at my watch. It was 3:35. According to Ricky, I was supposed to work with Annie from 3:30 to 4:30. When she first told me, I thought that sounded okay. The buses ran every fifteen minutes, so I could take the 4:45 home.

Now, however, the plan seemed to have a few holes in it.

Oh, boy, I thought. This is going to be the longest hour of my life.

I decided to try a different approach.

"Okay, Annie," I said, sounding surprisingly patient. "Here's the deal. I'm supposed to hang out with you for an hour. How about if we try it, just this once? An hour out of your life isn't going to kill you. All you have to do is sit down and give me a chance to get to know you. . . ."

"What do you know about kids, anyway?"

"Me?" I blinked. She had me there. I didn't really know very much about kids at all. At least, that was my first thought. Then I remembered that it hadn't been that long since I had been eight years old.

"I'll tell you what I know about kids," I said. "In fact, I'll show you."

I glanced around the library. It didn't take me long to find what I was looking for. I found the section with books for young readers and then headed right over. I knelt down in front of one of the shelves and began picking out books.

"What do you think you're doing?" Annie asked suspiciously. She moved a little closer.

"I want to introduce you to some friends of mine."

"Friends? What do you mean, friends? There's nobody in here but you and me."

"That's where the surprise comes in."

"Huh? What surprise?" By now, she had come right over to me. I could feel her standing behind me, watching me more closely.

I glanced over at her. "There are people in these pages, Annie. Wonderful people. Girls who are just like you. They like to do the same things you like to do. They feel the same way you feel. When I was eight years old, my best friends were in books. Now, if you'll let me, I'll help you get to know them, too."

Gently, I held out one of the books to her. It had been one of my favorites when I was about her age. I could remember spending the whole summer when I was eight years old, perched in an apple tree in our backyard, reading. This particular book, I had read over and over, pulling it off the shelf at those special times when I really needed a friend—a friend just like the main character in the book.

It was actually exciting, being able to pass on the experience. Which is why I was so astounded when Annie reached over and knocked it out of my hand. For the second time in the past five minutes, a book went flying across the library.

"Books are stupid!" She spat out her words. "School's stupid, too. What a waste of time!"

I was losing patience—fast. "Okay, then. What do you like, Annie?"

"I don't know."

"Isn't there anything you like to do?"

"I don't know."

I was getting desperate. "Do you like to . . . eat ice cream?"

"Why, so I can be fat like you?"

I felt as if she had just thrown another book at me. I just stared at her, my mouth open. It took me a few seconds to get my bearings. When I did, I was all set to give her a piece of my mind.

But it was too late. She was already heading out the door.

"This was the dumbest idea of all time," she called over her shoulder. "If you want to butt into other people's business, that's fine with me. Only do me a favor: go find somebody else to bother!"

And she was gone.

I plopped down on the floor of the library, then sat

there for a long time. I was trying to figure out what had just happened.

Was it me? I wondered. Did I say or do something to make Annie dislike me so much? Then I remembered that she had hit me with a book before I'd even gotten inside the library. So it *wasn't* my fault.

I suppose that should have made me feel better. Unfortunately, all it did was make the whole thing seem even worse. One by one, I put the books back on the shelf. Then I headed out to the bus stop. If I was lucky, I was thinking, maybe I could still catch the 3:45 back home.

chapter
six

"I thought this volunteer thing was supposed to make me feel better about myself, not *worse*," I muttered as I stuck my key into the back door of my house and went in.

It was late afternoon by then, and the sun was already pretty low in the sky. This long, grueling day was ending—finally. I looked forward to retreating to my warm, cozy house. To curling up in my warm, cozy room. Most of all, to being *alone*.

The house was quiet. Kelly was undoubtedly out somewhere with her friends, having more fun than I could even imagine. My father was still at work. Mom was the only one home. I could hear her upstairs, puttering around. The radio in her bedroom was on, turned to the classical music station she loves.

I was about to head for my room when I decided that what I really needed was a sympathetic ear. And two of the most sympathetic ears I knew of happened to be attached to the heads of the other members of the Bubble Gum Gang. I headed straight for the kitchen phone.

I dialed Samantha first. Busy signal. With a loud sigh, I tried Betsy. Another busy signal. It wasn't hard to figure out whom each of them was talking to. And I wouldn't have been the least bit surprised to find out that *what* they were talking about was *me*.

"So much for moral support," I mumbled.

Then I had another idea. It was inspired, at least in part, by the fact that I happened to be in the kitchen. Having a little snack: now *that* was what I considered a good way to cheer myself up. Immediately I began poking around inside the refrigerator. Nothing too interesting in there. Apples, oranges . . . nothing to get very excited about.

Next I tried the cabinets. There, among the cans of soup and boxes of macaroni, was an open bag of chocolate-chip cookies. My favorite kind, no less, the ones with nuts.

I froze, my heart skipping a beat. I thought of the oranges and apples in the refrigerator. Perfectly respectable foods, both of them. Very healthy. Very low in calories, with no fat at all. The ideal snack food . . . especially for a person watching her weight.

Still, this had been a particularly bad day. And I was really, really hungry. And these chocolate-chip cookies with the nuts were my favorites. These and a hundred other arguments roared in my head. Most of them debated the pros, rather than the cons, of helping myself to a few cookies.

I deserve them! I want them! I need them! the voices insisted. And then: how much damage could three or four cookies do?

They were all powerful arguments—or at least they seemed to be at the time. In fact, in the end they turned out to be indisputable. Quickly I took the package off the shelf, grabbed four cookies, and stuck them in my pocket.

Sure, I felt guilty. And I knew that in breaking my commitment to eating only healthy foods, foods that would help me reach my goal of slimming down, I was only hurting myself. But at that moment, the only thing that mattered to me was the terrible way I was feeling about myself . . . and the possibility that, for a few seconds, at least, wolfing down a fistful of sweets might just make that feeling go away.

Still, as I left the kitchen, I didn't exactly walk away; it was more like I *slunk* away. And I made a point of walking softly, since I didn't want my mother to know I'd come in. She is, after all, sharp enough to be able to pick up on the smell of chocolate coming from my pocket.

I never did make it to my bedroom. A second wave of inspiration hit. I bypassed the second floor entirely, instead heading straight for the attic. Up the ladder, through the trapdoor, back to the room that, amazingly enough, had once seemed forbidding.

What difference does it make if I don't have Samantha and Betsy around to make me feel better? I was thinking. I always have Charlotte.

And I didn't have to worry about getting a busy signal. All I had to do was move the stack of photo albums, open up the trunk, and take out the diary. I scrunched up a blanket to make a sort of seat for myself, pushed it next to the window, and got comfortable. Munching on the first chocolate-chip cookie, I opened the book up to the page I had marked with the folded-up treasure map, the exact spot where I had left off. It was dated September 8, 1912.

"Dear Diary," the entry began. "Today I went back to school. . . ."

It was only a question of seconds before I was transported back in time once again. There I was, walking side by side with Charlotte once again, living her life right along with her.

This time, instead of happily carrying on for page after page about her glorious summer vacation, Charlotte's writing had an entirely different tone. It didn't take long before her matter-of-fact reports of what her new teachers were like and which books she was looking forward to reading gave way to something entirely different.

"Dear Diary," she had written on October 2. "Oh, it's just too awful for words! I can't believe this is happening all over again. And here I'd been hoping that this year would be different. That now that I'd turned twelve, things would be better. Instead, I found out today that even though I feel like *I'm* growing up, not everybody else is."

I leaned forward, squinting in the fading light from the window. The sun was going down quickly, but I didn't want to stop reading even long enough to switch on the attic light.

"I was coming out of school this afternoon, minding my own business, thinking about nothing more important than how heavy my schoolbooks were. All of a sudden Danny Tucker rode by on his bicycle and yelled, 'Skinny Minnie! Skinny Minnie!'

"I was so surprised I nearly dropped my books— and the road was all muddy from yesterday's rain. Yes, that would have been awful. But the awfulness of that would have been nothing compared to how awful I was feeling as Danny rode off, laughing to himself as if he were the most clever boy who every lived."

I nearly dropped the diary. Charlotte . . . *too thin*? Was it possible that she had gone through the same kind of teasing—even ridicule—that I went through, and all because she was too skinny?

I didn't know if I felt like laughing or crying. Laughing because of this odd coincidence I had just stumbled upon, something shared by me and this girl who had lived almost a century earlier. Crying because she, too, had been hurt by having the bad luck to look a certain way, a way that not everybody approved of.

I closed the diary and reached for the photograph album. Up until now, I hadn't really taken the time to study the pictures in it. I'd figured I'd get around to it when I was ready. Now, suddenly, I was ready.

I was actually nervous as I opened the album. There was the black-and-white portrait of Charlotte I had seen the day I'd first found her trunk. The picture that had caught me by surprise because of the great resemblance between her and me. This time, I kept turning pages.

Most of the pictures were black-and-white. The others were a strange sepia tone that I'd seen in other photographs, usually in places like museums. It was hard to believe that the people in these pictures were actually my relatives. Some of them, anyway. As I flipped through the pages, I was frustrated by the fact that I had no idea who most of these people were.

Still, I studied them all. There were family gatherings, where everybody sat around a big table laden down with food. Groups of teenagers gathered at the side of a lake, wearing old-fashioned bathing suits that looked so ridiculous they made me laugh out loud. People standing together awkwardly in twos and threes, looking very self-conscious about having their picture taken.

No, I couldn't identify everyone. But I could always pick out Charlotte. I knew her face as well as I knew my own.

And the thing that struck me about every one of the pictures was that she wasn't *that* skinny.

Sure, she was thin. The kind of thinness that, these days, people admire. Model-thin, like my sister Kelly. And I had to admit, most of the other girls in the photographs were a little rounder than Charlotte. But the differences were minimal.

The fact that she should have been singled out because of the fact that she was a teensy bit skinnier than everyone else was completely crazy.

I went back to the diary, hoping that the incident with creepy old Danny Tucker would turn out to be a one-shot deal. Instead, as I skimmed the next ten or twelve pages, I found out that poor Charlotte—my wonderful, lively, charming great-grandaunt—was an outsider. She wrote about walking home from school all alone, when all the other children at her school went home in groups. She wrote about feeling awkward at the harvest picnic that was held every October because she had nobody to sit with except her parents and her little brother.

When I came across a diary entry dated November 15, almost the exact same date, only slightly more than eighty years earlier, I saw that the writing was blurred. Was it possible that Charlotte had been crying as she wrote about the birthday party being planned by the most popular girl at school . . . an event that she'd just learned she hadn't been invited to?

I slammed the diary shut. I took a few deep breaths, wanting to keep my own tears from falling. Poor Charlotte! Couldn't she see that, no matter what the others thought, she was a very special person? For a moment, I found myself longing to go back in time. If only I had lived when Charlotte lived, I would have been her friend. I would have convinced her that she was worthwhile. If only . . . if only . . .

"You're really getting into this, aren't you?"

I jumped. Turning around quickly, I half expected to see a ghost . . . Charlotte's ghost. Instead, there was Kelly, poking her head up through the trap door.

"I thought Mom said you didn't have to do any more cleaning until the weekend," she said. "I know I have no plans to go back down to that filthy old basement until Mom positively forces me to."

"Oh . . . well, I . . ." I was having trouble focusing on the present. Part of me was still back there with Charlotte, furious with the girl who hadn't invited her to that special birthday party. But Kelly's presence was a strong reminder that I belonged in *this* decade, not Charlotte's. "This is such a dirty job that I'm anxious to get it out of the way."

Kelly wrinkled her nose. "I can see what you mean. By the way, I think you're the hands-down winner of our contest."

I frowned. "Contest?"

"Sure. The one about who was going to meet up

with more spiders, you or me. I'd say you definitely won."

"I haven't seen a single spider up here," I insisted. "Actually, working all alone up here in the attic has turned out to be kind of fun."

Kelly just gave me an odd look. "I just wanted to tell you that if you can bring yourself to leave this wonderful place, dinner's almost ready. Don't expect too much, though. Tonight was my turn to cook."

That meant spaghetti. Kelly always made spaghetti. It was the only thing she could make. After all, the only skills it takes are the ability to boil water, to open a box, and—the really tricky part—to open a jar of tomato sauce and heat it up.

"I'll make a salad," I offered. "Just give me a minute to finish up here."

"Sure." Kelly shrugged, meanwhile giving me another one of her strange looks, the kind that said she secretly suspected that her little sister was actually from another planet. Then she disappeared down the ladder.

I was reluctant to leave Charlotte. But I did have my own life to lead. I tucked the diary back into the trunk along with the photograph album. Once again, I found myself talking—even though nobody was around to hear me.

"I have to go now," I whispered, "but I'll be back."

It wasn't until I started down the ladder that I realized I'd forgotten to eat the other three cookies.

"You know, it's funny," I said casually over dinner. "I've lived here in Hanover all my life, yet there's still so much about this town that I just don't know."

Twirling my spaghetti, I looked around the table. The other three members of the Farrell family were absorbed in doing that same twirling motion. It was actually pretty funny.

But at the moment, I was looking for information, not entertainment.

"I'm kind of an old-timer here myself," my father volunteered. "Don't forget, I was born and raised in this town."

That, I knew only too well. After all, Charlotte had been his grandfather's sister ... and she, too, had lived in Hanover. I was the fourth generation of Farrells to grow up here. But that hardly made me an expert.

"I know, Dad. And that's why I thought maybe you could help me out with something."

"I'd be glad to."

I took a deep breath. I never liked making things up, especially where my family was concerned. But when it came to Charlotte and her diary and the poem filled with clues to where her treasure had been buried, I still felt that same need to protect our little eighty-year-old secret.

"I wonder what churches were around in—oh, I don't know, say 1912."

"The year 1912?" Kelly gave me another one of those sister-from-another-planet looks. "What on earth do you want to know that for?"

"Maybe it's a school project," said my mother, helping herself to more salad.

Thank you, Mom. "That's right!" I cried. "Mom hit it on the nose. It is for a school project. A project on, uh, old buildings in Hanover."

"Nineteen-twelve, huh?" My father leaned back in his chair. "That's a tough one."

"I bet I know," said my mother. "How about the Old Church?"

"Of course!" I snapped my fingers. Why hadn't I thought of that? "That white church, over on the corner behind the park."

"What year was it built?" asked Kelly. I don't think she was really interested; I think she was just trying to be part of the conversation.

"I'm not exactly sure," said my father. "But with a name like the Old Church, you figure it's got to be . . . well, old."

"That's not it's real name, Daddy!" Kelly cried, laughing.

"No," said my mother. "But that is what everybody calls it. I'd say that if you're looking for the oldest church in town, that's got to be it."

"Thanks," I said. I was ready to move on to other

topics. My family, however, happened to find the subject of old things fascinating.

"Speaking of relics," said my mother, "I noticed you were up in the attic again. I appreciate your dedication, Carla. I never expected you to get so involved in something as deadly as cleaning the attic."

I shrugged. "Just trying to do my part."

"Speaking of doing your part," my sister said, her face lighting up, "I heard an interesting rumor at school today."

"Now Kelly," my mother scolded, "you know it's not a good idea to go around spreading rumors."

"Oh, I'm not spreading this one around. I'm just trying to find out if it's true or not. You see, it happens to be about Carla."

"Carla?" both my parents said at the same time.

As I glanced up, I could feel my face growing warm. I had a sudden feeling that the spaghetti sauce wasn't the only thing at this table that was bright red.

"I heard you volunteered for Help, Unlimited," Kelly went on matter-of-factly. "One of the girls in my gym class is a volunteer there, and she told me she saw your name on some list."

"How wonderful!" Mom cried. "Is that true, Carla?"

I just nodded.

"Good for you!" my father exclaimed. "But I'm puzzled. Why didn't you tell us?"

Because I was forced into it by my two best

friends, I was tempted to say. And because my very first session as a volunteer was a total disaster. *And* because I have absolutely no intention of doing anything like that ever again.

"Oh, I'm not sure it's going to work out yet," I said lightly. "I didn't want to say anything until I found out more about it."

"Well, let us know if you hear anything," my mother urged. "We're really proud of you, Carla."

I was just wishing I could disappear under the table somewhere when I had a minor brainstorm. Smiling politely at my sister, I said, "How about you, Kelly? Ever think of doing something like that? Help, Unlimited could probably use somebody like you."

My plan worked. For the rest of the meal, my parents tried talking Kelly into being as good-hearted a person as her little sister was. I, meanwhile, was left alone to think about the Old Church, the white building behind the park. And to try to figure out when my first chance to go exploring there was going to be.

chapter
seven

It was drizzling as I hurried through the doors of good old Hanover Junior High School the following morning. Clearly it was going to be another one of those depressing gray days. In fact, as I hurried to my locker, I was wondering what cruel person had invented November in the first place.

Suddenly, another thought popped into my mind. It occurred to me that maybe, just maybe, Betsy and Samantha wouldn't be as sympathetic about the terrible experience I'd had with Annie Cooper as I hoped. After all, volunteering for Help, Unlimited *had* been their idea in the first place.

As I sat in homeroom, I found myself dreading first-period English class. All three of us—Betsy, Sam, and me—were in that class. As a matter of fact, it's where we first met. Already I could hear the pep talk they would probably give me. It was playing in my head as if I were wearing an invisible Walkman.

"You simply need a way to approach Annie," Betsy, the practical one, would say. "I have an idea. How about if we all meet at the library after school? We can read every book on child psychology we can find. Surely the Bubble Gum Gang can find *some* way to solve the Mystery of Uncooperative Annie."

Samantha, meanwhile, would probably take a less intellectual approach. Something gentler . . . and much more emotional.

"You need to give her time, Carla," she would tell me. "Annie needs to learn that she can trust you. First you have to prove to her that you really do want to be her friend. Then you'll start to see some progress. All you need is a little patience."

Who knows? Maybe those arguments could even turn out to be sensible, I thought.

But it hardly mattered. Given the way I was feeling about the whole Annie Cooper nightmare, I wasn't about to stick around to find out.

So I sort of slunk into Mr. Homer's English class. "Pretend you're invisible," I told myself as I edged into my seat, my eyes fixed on the floor. "I'm a pretty good actress. Maybe if I *act* like they can't see me . . ."

So much for the power of positive thinking.

"Carla!" both Sam and Betsy shrieked the moment I settled into my seat.

"How was it?" Betsy cried.

"Tell us every single detail," Samantha demanded.

"Don't tell me—it was great."

"I bet Annie Cooper loved you, right?"

I looked from Betsy to Sam and back to Betsy. Both girls' faces were lit up like one hundred watt light bulbs. "To tell you the truth," I said, "it was one of the worst experiences of my entire life."

They both looked so disappointed that for a few seconds I regretted telling them. Then I remembered that they were the ones who'd gotten me into this in the first place.

"Look," I said, holding up my hands before they had a chance to offer any of that well-meaning advice I was expecting. "I'm just not cut out for this kind of thing, okay? Everybody has special talents. Mine happen to be acting and baking brownies. So what if I'm not the answer to every one of Annie Cooper's problems? Surely you've heard that old saying: You can't win 'em all."

By this point, Samantha and Betsy looked like they were going to burst. I just knew they were dying to start trying to talk me into giving it a second chance. I looked around, hoping our teacher would get started on time for a change. But Mr. Homer was nowhere to be seen.

Here goes, I thought, bracing myself.

"You have to give it more time!" Betsy insisted.

Samantha was nodding away. "You can't become someone's friend in one short hour. How can you give up before you've even given it a fighting chance?"

"First of all, I'm not supposed to become Annie Cooper's friend," I reminded them. "I'm supposed to find a way to help her. To get through to her. To work on her problems, whatever they are."

More to myself than to them, I added, "So far, it seems that her main problem could be solved by getting her a job as a pitcher on the baseball team."

"You need to find a better way, that's all," said Betsy. "I'll tell you what. How about if, right after school, we all head over to the library so we can—"

"Thanks, but I already have plans for after school." In response to Sam and Betsy's confused stares, I added, "The diary? The treasure map?"

"Oh, Carla," Betsy groaned. "You're not still wasting your time with that silly old treasure map, are you?"

I just looked at her. "Can this really be happening? Is it possible that a member of the Bubble Gum Gang, dedicated to the fine art of solving mysteries, is actually referring to a *treasure map*—one that's nearly a century old, I might add—as *silly*?" Dramatically I clutched my heart.

"It think what Betsy means," Samantha said with great patience, "is that it might turn out to be more rewarding for you if you put your time into something like helping Annie Cooper than . . . well, you know."

By then, Mr. Homer had come into the classroom. He was talking to some of the other students. I kept wishing class would start. Instead, he was debating the hot topic of which one of Edgar Allan Poe's short stories is scarier, "The Tell-Tale Heart" or "The Murders in the Rue Morgue."

"The treasure map is important to me," I retorted. "In fact, it would be nice if the two of you were willing to help me figure it out. I've already made some progress, zeroing in on the first clue. I asked my parents which church is the oldest in town, and they steered me toward the Old Church. And that's precisely where I intend to start.

"Besides," I added, trying to sound casual, "maybe the clues in the poem will lead us to a real treasure. Ever think of that?"

Betsy, I could tell, was getting impatient. I thought she was about to light into me. So I was especially surprised by what she came out with next.

"Okay, Carla. I'll make a deal with you."

My eyebrows shot up in astonishment. "A deal?"

"That's right. Here it is: If you agree to stick with Help, Unlimited a little bit longer—if you agree to keep seeing Annie, at least for a little while—Sam and I will help you find the treasure."

I blinked. "Really?" I looked over at Samantha. She looked a little surprised at first, but then she nodded.

"Count me in," she said seriously.

I just stared. "This Annie Cooper thing is that important to you?"

More nodding.

"Well, okay then. It's a deal."

Wouldn't you know that Mr. Homer, the king of bad timing, would choose that moment to start class.

"All right, everybody," he said, picking up a piece of chalk. "Let's all take out our copies of *The Stories of Edgar Allan Poe*. Betsy, we'll start with you. What was your impression of the famous mystery story, 'The Murders in the Rue Morgue'?"

It wasn't easy, concentrating on somebody else's mystery. Not when I knew that one of my own was now lurking just around the corner.

Just as I'd expected, the Old Church was deserted late on a Wednesday afternoon. It was still drizzling, the light, cold rain adding to the discomfort everyone was already feeling as we headed toward the desolate church grounds. The sky was also beginning to darken, partly because it was so late, partly because of the clouds that were growing even thicker.

"You know what I wish I were doing right now?" Betsy mumbled as she followed me and Samantha up the front walk that led to the building's main entrance.

"I bet it has something to do with being indoors," Samantha called over her shoulder.

"It sure does. It also has something to do with fire-

places. And hot chocolate. And a good, juicy book—
the kind that lets you get lost in its pages."

"Come on, you two!" I said heartily. "Where's
your sense of adventure?"

"I left mine home, in front of the fireplace," replied Samantha.

"This is our first real treasure hunt!" I reminded
them. "Just think: almost a century ago, someone
buried treasure back here. And we're about to find
it!"

"Assuming it's still there," said Betsy. "After all, a
century is a long, long time."

"Betsy's right," Samantha added. "It's bad enough
you're dragging us out in this cold . . . in the rain . . .
in the dark. But to think we're out here looking for a
buried treasure that's probably not even there
anymore . . ."

"We have to try," I said. "We have to give it our
best shot."

"Why?" Betsy and Samantha asked in unison.

"Because we're the Bubble Gum Gang, that's
why!"

By that point we had reached the front of the
church. I peeked out from under the hood of my yellow slicker to look at the poem one more time.

"Okay. So far, so good. 'Where voices sing a gentle song, Where faces lift toward heaven . . .' "

"We know that part," Samantha said impatiently,

pulling her rain hat down over her head. "What's next?"

" 'Where sunlight streams through colored glass, behind, to number seven . . .' "

"We have to go around back," Betsy said. "And we have to look for something that there's seven of. Like trees or flower beds or fence posts."

"After that, we're supposed to look for some stones, right?" asked Samantha.

"Right." I read from the poem again. " 'There, upon the earth so green are stones that last and last.' "

Betsy looked at Samantha and sighed. "Let's get this over with."

We trudged around the side of the church. Not surprisingly, there was no sidewalk there, not even a path. Most people walk *into* churches, after all, not around them. What it all added up to was three pairs of feet caked with thick, gloppy mud.

"Next time I go on a treasure hunt," Betsy muttered, "remind me to wear boots."

But I barely paid attention. "Look!" I cried, pointing. "Bushes! There's a whole row of them."

"I wouldn't call that a *row*, exactly," Samantha observed, looking doubtful.

"So what if they don't line up perfectly?" I insisted. "I just have a feeling that's what the 'seven' refers to. Let's figure out which one is the seventh.

According to the poem, that's where we'll find the stones that 'last and last.' ''

"Carla," Betsy said slowly, "I don't want to disappoint you or anything, but I don't think these teensy-weensy bushes look eighty years old."

"Betsy's right," Samantha echoed. "Actually, they look more like *eight* years old."

"Maybe . . . maybe they replace them every few years," I said. I had already grown much too excited to let anything like common sense get in my way. "This has *got* to be it. Come on, let's find number seven."

Betsy opened her mouth to say something. But she changed her mind. Instead, she just shrugged, then followed behind.

"One, two, three . . ." I counted aloud, following the haphazard scattering of scrubby little bushes. My heart was pounding away like crazy. I was getting close to the treasure; I could feel it. This *had* to be right. So far, everything fit right into place. In another few minutes, I would be at the spot where the treasure was hidden. And it had to be there; it simply had to.

"Here's number seven!" I cried, looking back at my friends triumphantly. I was standing next to a sad-looking little bush no more than two feet high.

Samantha let out a deep sigh as she looked it over. "Okay, what comes next?"

I checked the poem. " 'There upon the earth so green . . .' "

"It looks kind of brown, if you ask me," Betsy grumbled.

" 'Are stones that last and last. Find the oldest on the hill. Face east, and travel past . . .' "

"Wait a minute. The *oldest*? How on earth are we supposed to figure out which one of these is the oldest?" Samantha had crouched down in the wet, muddy soil. She was examining the hundreds, if not thousands, of stones that were mixed in with the dirt.

"Maybe whoever wrote the poem just threw this part in to confuse us," Betsy suggested. After a moment, she added, "It seems to be working."

"Maybe what matters here is facing east," said Samantha.

"Good point." I glanced at the poem once again. "We're supposed to 'face east and travel past to the valley down below.' "

"East is that way," Betsy said, pointing.

I was filled with hope as I looked in the direction in which she was pointing. And immediately my heart sank about two feet.

Sure, there was a sort of valley down below. Actually, it was more like a flat stretch of land that kind of sloped downward. That was the good news.

The bad news was that it was completely paved over.

"A parking lot!" Samantha cried. "There's nothing there but concrete!"

"And a lot of cars," Betsy added ruefully. "I'm so sorry, Carla."

"So much for the treasure hunt," I mumbled. I forced myself to smile. Then, with a shrug, I said, "Oh, well. You win some, you lose some."

There was no fooling Betsy and Samantha. Sam came over and slung her arm around my shoulders—even though they were sopping wet.

"Carla, are you okay? You must be so disappointed!"

"I'm fine, really." Same fake smile, same high-pitched voice. "What do you say we call it quits? Let's go home."

Betsy looked at me sadly, shaking her head.

"I feel like the Bubble Gum Gang let you down," she said in a soft voice.

"It's not the Bubble Gum Gang's fault," I assured her, still sounding a whole lot cheerier than I felt. "It's just that eighty years is a long time, that's all."

As I stood there in the rain, with cold water snaking down the back of my neck and oozing into my shoes, I felt completely defeated. And knowing that the treasure hunt had led to a dead end was only part of it.

The other part was the deal I had made with Betsy and Samantha. They had followed through on their end, helping me follow the clues in the poem. Now, it was time for me to come across with my part. Annie Cooper and I were still a team.

It would have been hard to say which of those two things was making me feel worse.

chapter
eight

"You again! And here I was sure I'd seen the last of you."

It was Friday after school, and I'd just strode into the Millard Fillmore Elementary School library to find Annie Cooper standing in the middle of the big room. Once again her arms were folded across her chest. Her chin was stuck into the air, and she was wearing the same don't-mess-with-me look she'd been wearing the last time around.

What I felt like saying was, I thought you'd seen the last of me, too.

But I didn't. Instead, I kept thinking about the deal I had made with Samantha and Betsy. They had come across with their end, and now it was time for me to come across with mine.

As I stood face-to-face with Annie, my stomach sinking somewhere down around the carpet, I could have kicked myself for having ever made that deal. In fact, I could just as easily have kicked myself for making that first phone call to Help, Unlimited.

Still, there I was. And there Annie was. I had to do *something*. So I decided to give it my best shot.

"Annie," I said, trying desperately not to let my nervousness show, "today is the most important day of your life."

She didn't smile. Or even look curious. Instead, she peered at me suspiciously. Still, at least I'd gotten her attention.

"I am about to introduce you to someone wonderful. Someone who may well change your life."

"Oh, yeah?" She looked interested for about a zillionth of a second. Then she scowled.

"Oh, I know. You're talking about some stupid character in some stupid book, right? That's this really important person you plan to 'introduce' me to?"

"Nope." I sat down at one of the tables scattered throughout the library. It was very low to the ground, the kind that's specially made for children. The chairs were tiny, too. I felt like a giant.

But I was acting very casual as I made myself comfortable. I made a point of dramatically plopping the book bag I'd brought smack in the middle of the table. I gestured toward it with my chin.

"He's in there."

"Who's in there?"

Through the corner of my eye I could see Annie edging closer. But I kept looking at the book bag.

"I get the creeps just thinking about him," I went on, pretending to shudder.

By now Annie had come over to the table. "What have you got in there? A snake?"

"No. Something worse."

She looked skeptical. Folding her arms across her chest, she said, "A lizard, right?"

"This guy's about a billion times worse than a lizard."

"I know. A rat."

Finally, I looked her right in the eye. "The master of horror. The king of terror. The one person who has come face-to-face with evil—and looked it straight in the eye."

Annie still looked like she didn't quite believe me. But at least she glanced over at the book bag and said, "Oh, yeah? Let's see."

Calling upon my best acting skills, I reached toward the book bag with great drama. By this point, even I was scared. Slowly I opened the flap. I reached in . . . and pulled out my book of scary stories by Edgar Allan Poe.

"A book!" Annie scoffed. "For a minute there I thought you had something *good* in there."

"Oh, but this *is* good. Annie, have you ever read the story 'The Tell-Tale Heart'?"

"What's that?"

I gave her a long, cool look. "On second thought, I don't know if you're old enough for this."

"I'm old enough!" she insisted.

"Well, maybe . . . But how do I know you're brave enough?"

"You think I'm a scaredy-cat? No way. I'm not afraid of anything."

"Okay, if that's the case, then maybe you really are ready for this." I picked up the book gingerly. "I sure hope so."

I picked up the book and started to read. For the second time that day, I thanked my lucky stars that acting was something I was good at.

I put everything I had into reading that story aloud. Every once in a while I snuck a peek at Annie, just to make sure she was listening. She was. Who wouldn't be enthralled by Edgar Allan Poe's masterful tale of a man who commits murder, then buries the body underneath the floorboards of the bedroom, only to be driven to confessing because of the loud, endless beating of the victim's heart?

When I was done, I looked at her and said, "So? What did you think?"

She shrugged. "It was okay. I guess."

Not the most enthusiastic review of all times. Still, I was thrilled that I'd managed to hold Annie's interest for such a long time. But I felt like I was doing all the work, and I wanted her to get involved. This was a two-way street, after all. Besides, I was getting a sore throat from having read aloud for so long.

I closed the book and handed it to her. "Now it's your turn."

"What?"

"I read you a story. Now you read me a story."

She looked at the book as if it really were a snake or a rat. "No way. Reading's for nerds."

"What are you talking about?" I cried. "Reading is *not* for nerds. It's for everybody. It's wonderful. It's . . . it's . . ."

I was quickly getting the feeling I was losing Annie. And now that I had her, at least a little bit, that was the last thing I wanted to do.

"Don't you want to read about a bunch of murders nobody could solve? There's this really cool story in here called 'The Murders in the Rue Morgue.' I don't want to ruin it by giving the ending away, but it turns out that the murderer wasn't even *human*."

I expected her to look impressed. Instead, she slid the book back over in my direction. "You read it."

"Annie, I'm getting hoarse. I really don't think—"

"*You* read it," she insisted.

I was starting to get tired of this. But I didn't want it to show.

"Okay, I have another idea," I said. "How about if you read me a story that you particularly like?"

"That sounds boring."

"Oh, you'd be surprised. Where are your school-books?"

"Over there." Halfheartedly, she pointed to another library table, one that was halfway across the room.

"Fine. I'll go check them out." I went over to her books and looked through them. A math book, a science book . . . and just as I'd expected, a book of stories. I figured she'd be much more comfortable reading something like this, a book geared toward her age group's reading level.

"Here," I said, handing her the book. "Pick out a story you really like and—"

"I don't *want* to read. I hate books!" With one fast swing of her arm, Annie knocked the book off the table.

"Oh, boy," I muttered. "This is where I came in."

I was ready to give it up. But Annie, I quickly found out, was just beginning.

"Who asked you to come here anyway?" she shrieked. "I don't want you here! I don't want any special favors from anybody."

Calmly, I reached down and picked up the book. As I did, I noticed something strange about it.

"Annie," I said slowly, "have you actually read this book?"

"Of course I did," she shot back. "My dumb old teacher is always giving us stuff to read in there. And it's all boring, every bit of it."

I was about to ask another question, about why this

book looked brand new, as if it'd never even been opened, if she used it in school all the time.

And then something clicked. Somewhere, deep inside my brain, all the pieces of this weird puzzle I'd been agonizing over fit together. I suddenly understood why Annie's grades were so poor, why she was such a behavior problem . . . why she was so angry.

Annie Cooper couldn't read.

The first time I'd sat in the waiting room at Help, Unlimited's headquarters, I'd been wondering what on earth I was doing there. This time, as I perched on the edge of my chair, barely paying attention to the posters tacked up on the walls, I knew *exactly* what I was doing. I had a good reason. A purpose. A goal.

In fact, you might even say I had a mission.

And so the nervousness I was feeling was also very different from what I'd felt the first time around. This time, I was anxious because I couldn't wait to tell Ricky Norris what I'd discovered—and I couldn't wait to hear what she'd have to say about it.

When she finally appeared in the doorway, I jumped out of my chair.

"I have to talk to you," I said breathlessly.

She chuckled. "So I figured."

Once we were in her office, it only took her a few seconds to settle in behind her desk. Meanwhile, I was still sitting on the edge of my chair. In fact, it was all I could do to stay in it.

"Ms. Norris," I told her the moment she looked at me expectantly, "I finally figured out what makes Annie Cooper tick." My words came rushing out like Niagara Falls. "Even better than that: I know why she's having such a hard time at school."

Her response was a quick nod. "Go on," she said patiently. Her eyes were fixed on me as if she were waiting for me to say something really important. And I was ready to do just that.

I took a deep breath. "Annie Cooper can't read. Yes, I know she's eight years old, and by that point most kids have become pretty good readers. But somehow she's fallen through the cracks."

I was expecting Ricky to look shocked. Or even to look at me like I was from another planet, coming up with an idea like that. Instead, she didn't look surprised at all.

"That would certainly explain a lot." She thought for a few seconds. "Yes, from what I know of her problems and her past behavior, I'd say there's a good chance you've hit the nail on the head."

My mouth dropped open. "You mean . . . you mean I'm right?"

"You certainly could be. You've met with Annie twice so far, right? So I assume that by now you've talked with her enough to get to know her. And that you've learned enough about her to come up with this conclusion. Now let's go back to the beginning."

I told her the whole story. As embarrassing as it

was, I even told her the part about Annie throwing a book at me before I'd even had a chance to say hello. I went on to explain what'd happened when I tried to get her to read the Edgar Allan Poe story to me. Ricky just listened, nodding every once in a while to show she was following what I was saying.

"So that's what happened," I finally said, leaning back in my chair and letting out a sigh. "What do you think?"

"I think Annie Cooper needs someone to teach her how to read."

I was feeling pretty good about myself. I had solved the Mystery of Annie Cooper! I could hardly wait to tell the other members of the Bubble Gum Gang.

In fact, running off to Betsy's or Sam's to share my thrilling news was exactly what I was thinking about. Now that Ricky knew Annie Cooper's problem, I was sure she'd want to turn her over to an expert. An English teacher, maybe, or someone who had been specially trained in teaching reading. So what she said next totally caught me off guard—so much so that I nearly toppled off my chair.

"When can you start?"

I looked at her, blinking a few times. "Excuse me?"

"I said, When can you start? Teaching Annie how to read, I mean."

"Ms. Norris, I don't know how to teach someone how to read!"

"Of course not. Not yet, anyway." She was shuffling through a stack of papers on her desk, looking for something. "Here it is. Everything you'll need to know."

"Everything I'll need to know about *what*?"

"About the literacy training program." Matter-of-factly she handed me a booklet. "You're in luck. The next training session begins in just two weeks."

"Wait a minute," I protested, holding up my hands. "Even if I *could* learn how to teach her how to read, you don't really think Annie Cooper would *let* me, do you?"

There was this funny smile on Ricky Norris's face. "I guess you'll have your hands full over the next few days, trying to convince her."

"But . . . but how on earth am I ever going to do that?" Already I had visions of hundreds of books raining down on my head.

Ms. Norris leaned forward, wearing a very serious expression. "Carla," she said, "learning how to read could well be the single most important thing that ever happens in Annie Cooper's life. Without that basic skill, she's going nowhere.

"Whether you want to admit it or not, you've become a very important person in her life. Sure, just about anyone could teach Annie how to read. But *you* already have a head start. You've already developed a relationship with her. You're her friend. . . ."

"Hold on," I insisted, holding up my hands. "I wouldn't go that far."

"You know her well enough to see that she can't read, right?" Ms. Norris said gently. "You're the first person in her life who's taken the time to figure that out. The first person who's known her well enough to see what should have been clear to a dozen different people. Let's face it, Carla. You're the first person who ever *cared*."

I could see that Ricky Norris wasn't about to take no for an answer.

"Well . . . okay." I didn't know if I should feel thrilled or beaten down. "What do I do next?"

"First of all, we sign you up for this literacy training program." She reached for the pamphlet. "It meets at the public library on Saturday mornings. I'll contact the organization, if you like. I'm pretty sure I can get you in, even though it is late."

I nodded. I could tell there was more.

"In the meantime," she went on, "it's your job to convince Annie that she can trust you. And that you want to help her. Before you can teach her to read, you need her cooperation."

"Great," I muttered. "And how am I supposed to do *that*?"

Ms. Norris was smiling. "Carla, you've come far

in a very short time. I have a feeling that if anybody can reach Annie Cooper, it's you."

If only I could have felt some of her optimism! Instead, as I sat there, I had this awful feeling that I had already gotten in over my head.

Speaking of heads, I thought with a sigh, maybe I'd better start wearing a helmet.

chapter
nine

"This is the hardest thing I've ever had to do in my entire life!" I wailed.

It was later that same day. The Bubble Gum Gang was having its usual Friday night hang-out session, celebrating the end of another long, grueling week of school.

This time, we were at Samantha's house. And that meant the three of us were lounging around in the lap of luxury. In addition to having her own phone in her room, Sam also has a television, a VCR, and a super-duper CD player that makes you feel like you're right on stage with the rock groups, hiding behind the drums. The room itself looks like something out of a magazine. Matching curtains, bedspread and lampshade, a rocking chair that's easily the most comfortable in the entire world . . . even a window seat.

As always, there were lots of snacks around—all of them healthy. I found myself missing the good old days of potato chips and chocolate bars. But I didn't dare suggest that we take a little break from our diet food, not with these two in the room. For now, I'd have to put my cravings for rich, sweet treats on hold. Instead, I concentrated on the popcorn. As I shoved handful after handful into my mouth, I pretended it was a hot fudge sundae in freeze-dried form.

I was supposed to be having fun. And all the ingredients were there. Yet none of it was helping my sour mood. Not the luxurious surroundings, not stuffing my face, not even having my two best friends there with me. From where I sat, all I could see was Annie Cooper's face—and the expression on it was anything but friendly.

"What am I supposed to do?" I went on. I wasn't exactly talking; it was more like I was moaning. "Somehow, I can't imagine prancing over to her front door, ringing the bell, and saying, 'Hello, Annie. I finally figured out that you don't know how to read, and that's why you're driving me and everybody else up the wall. But have no fear: Carla is here. I'll have you reading faster than you can say A-B-C.' "

"Carla," Samantha said gently, "maybe there's some way Betsy and I can help."

Betsy was quick to jump on the bandwagon. "That's a great idea! We'll do whatever you want us to do, Carla. Just say the word."

"The word is, 'Find a way to get me out of this.' "
Another fistful of popcorn found its way into my
mouth.

"I have an idea," Betsy went on. "Maybe we really
should go over to Annie's house and confront her
head-on."

" 'We'?" I repeated.

"That's right. It'll make it easier if all three of us
go." Betsy's green eyes were glowing with excite-
ment. "Samantha and I will wait outside while you
go in and talk to her. I have a feeling things will go
better on her own ground, instead of at her school library."

Samantha was nodding. "Excellent idea. Besides,
there's a good chance her parents will be on your
side. Once they find out what's going on with Annie,
I'm sure they'll be willing to help you out."

I could see where this was leading. Sure, it felt
good, having Sam and Betsy offer to come through
for me, just the way they always did. But there was
something else, something that was making the popcorn in my stomach feel like hundreds of little lead
balls.

These two were turning out to be just like Ricky
Norris, I realized. They believed in me. They really
thought I could do this.

And they weren't about to take no for an answer.

* * *

When I woke up Saturday morning, my first thought was that I needed a break from all the agonizing I'd been doing over Annie Cooper. Sure, I was committed to going over to her house later on that morning, with Samantha and Betsy cheering me on. But I had a few hours before that, and I desperately wanted a change of pace. I knew just where to go.

There was no good reason why I should go up to the attic to read Charlotte's diary. But I kept on doing it. Somehow, bringing it down to my bedroom and reading it there in bright daylight, surrounded by my sneakers and my posters of my favorite rock stars and all the symbols of living in the present just didn't fit with that long-ago world I was so anxious to go back to, at least for a little while. Besides, all Charlotte's other things were up there, as well: her dresses, her big straw hats with the silk flowers, the photograph albums.

There was one more reason. I was reluctant to share Charlotte's secret world with anyone—even the Bubble Gum Gang. Sure, I'd shown them the poem that doubled as a treasure map. I'd had to; otherwise, how could they have helped me try to solve it? But even doing that had been difficult. I really wanted to keep all this for myself. Charlotte's diary—in fact, everything about her—was just too special for me to bring myself to share it with anybody.

Still, it wasn't the diary I found myself reaching

for first. It was the treasure map in the form of a poem. Sure, I'd completely memorized it by this point. And I knew that when I tried to follow its clues, I'd met up with nothing but a dead end. Still, I couldn't help reading it over and over again. I kept hoping that if I looked at it enough, sooner or later something—*anything*—would strike me, some clue that I hadn't seen before.

By that point, Samantha and Betsy were both convinced that it was a lost cause. Tromping around the Old Church—in the rain, no less—was something I suspected they'd be kidding me about for years. If I'd had any sense, I would have forgotten all about the silly puzzle. I knew that . . . in my mind, anyway. In my heart, I just couldn't let it go. I simply *had* to solve the puzzle. I had to find out what the treasure was. I had to know what it was that mattered to Charlotte's grandmother more than anything on earth, what it was that was the treasure she most loved and, for her, had the greatest worth.

As usual, I saw nothing nothing new in those same words I had said to myself over and over again, about a jillion times. Discouraged, I turned to the diary. I opened it up to the page I'd marked the last time.

I expected to find more reports of poor Charlotte being teased at school, followed by pages and pages of sorrowful writing about how terrible she felt about not being able to fit in. Yet as I read, my heart started to pound.

I had finally gotten to the part of the diary where she wrote about the treasure hunt!

It was dated November 16, 1913—almost *exactly* eighty years earlier. "Dear Diary," she began, as always. "Today, the most wonderful thing happened. Grandmother made a treasure hunt for me! Instead of simply drawing me a map or giving me a list of clues, she wrote a poem. The clues were hidden in it. When I asked her why she had done it, she simply smiled and said, 'It's my way of helping to keep you from feeling so bad about yourself.'

"I welcomed the chance to stop thinking about myself so much. So I couldn't wait to follow the map. Fortunately, it wasn't very difficult. It was clear from the beginning that the place to start was the old gray church."

"Right," I muttered. "The church. Before they turned the backyard into a parking lot, anyway."

"What a surprise it turned out to be! I found the treasure! It was exactly where Grandmother's poem said it would be. And when I turned around, she was standing there, waiting for me. I gave her a big hug. That was all I needed to do to say 'thank you.'

"I'm going to save the poem she wrote forever, so that I'll never forget the wonderful thing she did for me. When I told her that, she laughed and said she was glad. 'Let's leave the treasure there,' she suggested. 'That way, maybe one day it will help someone else.' "

"Huh?" I said under my breath. Anxiously I turned the page, looking for more, hoping something would explain what all that meant. But the next entry in the diary was dated December, and it was all about some Christmas party Charlotte went to.

"Wait a minute!" I cried aloud. I felt cheated. What did it all mean? The treasure was still there? Charlotte and her grandmother had left it there . . . to "help someone else"?

So it *was* still there. I wanted more desperately than ever to find it. Seeing this treasure had meant so much to Charlotte . . . yet I couldn't figure out how or why. I suddenly felt like I was going to crawl right out of my skin if I didn't get to the bottom of this puzzle—and *soon*.

I sat in the middle of the attic for a long time, just thinking. My brain was clicking away, about a mile a minute. Something was in there, some little thing that was nagging at me, something that wouldn't go away . . . but somehow, I just couldn't get hold of it. Something was wrong. Something was off. If only I could figure it out. . . .

And then, all of a sudden, it came to me. The church! Charlotte had referred to the "old church" as gray. I checked the diary; sure enough, that was exactly what she had written. The "old gray church." Yet the "Old Church" in town, the one where Sam and Betsy and I had gone hunting for buried treasure, was *white*.

Was it possible we'd been searching at the wrong church?

My heart was really pounding by that point. The sound of it was practically filling the attic as I thought as hard as I could. A gray church, an old gray church . . .

All of a sudden, there it was. Clear as a bell. Big as the nose on my face. The tumbledown building that by now was covered with vines, practically hidden on a plot of land overgrown with bushes and weeds. The old building on the corner of Greenlawn and Cedar. That had been a church . . . and it was gray.

Finally, I was going to be able to solve the puzzle. The treasure was still there. Charlotte and her grandmother had left it there for someone else to find, and that someone else was going to be me.

I promised myself that the very first chance I got, I was going to rush over there. Finally, the clues were falling into place. By the time the day was over, the treasure would be mine.

In the meantime, however, I had other things to deal with. Namely, the Case of the Book-Throwing Student. Samantha and Betsy and I had agreed to meet late that morning, around eleven. When we'd made the plan, it had sounded like a good idea to get it over with early in the day. Now that it was time to do it, however, I felt like midnight would have been a much better idea. Midnight . . . in the year 2003.

Still, I did have a way of getting myself out the door. I tucked the diary and the treasure map into my book bag before slinging it over my shoulder, telling myself that on the way home, the Bubble Gum Gang could make a quick stop—at the old *gray* church. Knowing that I was about to get to the bottom of the mysterious poem and uncover the hidden treasure, once and for all, helped me put the Annie Cooper business into perspective. Even if I ended up with another black-and-blue mark, I reasoned, this was still bound to end up being one of the most exciting days of my life.

Samantha and Betsy were waiting for me at the bus stop, exactly as we'd planned. They looked positively excited, as if they were about to embark on an adventure, not accompany a reluctant friend on a mission she was dreading.

"All set?" Sam asked cheerfully.

"I'd rather be on my way to a math test," I replied. "Or even to the dentist for a root canal."

"Just think, Carla!" Betsy said with that same chirping tone. "You may well be on the verge of changing someone's life. Opening the door to reading, the most important thing anyone can learn. . . ."

"Come to think of it," I said as I boarded the bus with Sam in front of me and Betsy behind me, "my dentist's office is right up the street. Maybe he's in this morning."

The bus ride was the same one I'd taken the other

two times, when I'd gone to the elementary school where Annie was a student. This time, the three of us rode even further. I'd gotten the Coopers' address from Ricky Norris, and their house was a few blocks past Millard Fillmore Elementary School.

We got off in front of a small grocery store. The neighborhood was pleasant enough; rows of small houses lined narrow streets. We walked a block or two before we finally turned down a side street, one whose sign matched the address I had scribbled on a small piece of paper.

"Well, this is where Annie lives," I announced, checking the fifth house on the left, Number Thirty-three. Actually, the house was hard to miss. It was the only one on the block that looked as if no one bothered to take care of it. It reminded me of one of those "before-and-after" articles in a magazine. They always show a bunch of people "before" they get all fixed up with makeup and a cool hairstyle, then "after," when they look like models. This house definitely had a "before" look.

The paint was kind of faded, but what was even more noticeable was that it was peeling in quite a few places. One of the windows right in front was cracked. The fence was broken; the gate had completely fallen off. Even the grass was mostly brown and stubby, a pretty sorry state even if it was November. Once again I checked the houses surrounding it. They were all the same type, but the others looked like their owners made a point of taking much better care of them.

"This house looks like nobody loves it," Samantha remarked sadly.

Betsy nodded. "It looks like nobody cares."

I had to agree. "Well, maybe Annie's parents are just . . . busy."

I was already losing interest. After all, I hadn't come all this way to talk about real estate. Taking a deep breath, I said, "Okay, you two. You've done a great job of getting me here. Now why don't you take a little stroll around the neighborhood while I go ring the Coopers' doorbell?" I made a face. "Given the way things usually go with Annie, I should be out in about fifteen seconds."

They both said "Good luck" about a quadzillion times, then took off. That left me standing in front of the Coopers', listening to my heart and feeling my stomach drop down somewhere around my knees.

"Might as well get this over with," I muttered. And I headed toward the front door.

Since it was Saturday morning, I figured there'd be a few people home. I know that in my house, that's a time my family usually hangs out together, puttering around and doing little chores. I knocked loudly, expecting Annie's mom or dad to come to the door. Instead, when the door finally opened, Annie herself was facing me.

Her look of surprise quickly gave way to one of annoyance. "What are *you* doing here?" she barked.

"I just came by to visit," I said. "Actually, that's not completely true. There's something I want to talk to you about. Um, do you think I could come in?"

She paused. "There's nobody here right now."

"Nobody?" I didn't even try to hide my surprise. What was an eight-year-old girl doing home all alone? She answered my question before I had a chance to wonder for too long.

"My mom and my dad are both working," she replied.

I was about to ask if there was a baby-sitter there, or maybe a relative. An older brother or sister, at least. But Annie had said she was alone, and I had no reason not to believe her.

"Well, can I come in anyway?"

She just shrugged, as if she didn't care one way or the other. In fact, she just turned away. I followed her inside.

"You know, Annie," I said slowly, trying to be really careful not to say the wrong thing, "I feel terrible that we've gotten off to such a bad start."

She just stared at me, without saying a word. But at least she stayed in the living room, instead of taking off the way she could have.

Besides, I was thinking, at least she hasn't thrown any books yet.

But then I noticed something really strange. As I

looked around the living room, I saw there wasn't a single book around. Not a magazine or a newspaper . . . not even a television program.

"Anyway," I went on, sitting down on the couch, dropping my book bag down next to me, "I hope that from now on we'll be able to work together a little better."

"Work together?" Annie repeated. She was leaning against the wall, way over on the other side of the room. "Whoever said anything about you and me working together?"

It was time for a heavy dose of patience. "Annie, you've got to believe that I really do want to help you. You know as well as I do that you're not doing very well in school. It's not only your schoolwork, either. It's the way you act in the classroom. Everybody can see there's something wrong."

"Why doesn't everybody just leave me alone?" she demanded. "None of this is anybody's business."

I opened my mouth to speak, even though I had no idea what I was going to say. So far, it seemed, I had done nothing but argue with Annie. I kept trying to convince her that there was a good reason why I was taking an interest in her, yet it was a losing battle. So far, nothing had worked. I needed to try something new, something different. . . .

All of a sudden, I had a brainstorm.

"Annie," I said, reaching into my book bag, "there's something I want to show you."

She groaned. "Oh, no! Not another one of your *friends*!"

"She's better than a friend. She was my great-grandaunt."

"Huh?"

"Her name was Charlotte. She was born at the turn of the century. But Annie, even though she lived almost a century ago, she was so much like me!"

I was growing excited as I opened up the diary. Once again, I was getting caught up in another time . . . Charlotte's time. Only this time, being there was even better. This time, I wanted to bring Annie along with me.

"Oh, Annie, you've got to let me share this with you. Charlotte lived in a wonderful era, when girls like you and me wore dresses down below their knees and big floppy bows in their hair and huge straw hats. . . . And they rolled hoops and went to Sunday school picnics where they ate homemade ice cream from an old-fashioned freezer that had to be cranked by hand. . . ."

Maybe the things I was saying really did sound interesting to Annie. Or maybe it was just that I was so excited about them that my enthusiasm was contagious. At any rate, Annie eased across the room, peered over my shoulder, and looked down into the pages of Charlotte's diary.

"Look!" I cried, pointing to a page. "Here's the section about her first day of school. A boy rode by on his bicycle and made fun of her for being too skinny."

"Too skinny!" Annie cried. "That's crazy! Why would anybody make fun of somebody for being skinny?"

I shrugged. "People make fun of me for being fat."

"That's crazy, too!" Suddenly Annie seemed to remember that she, for one, could count herself as one of those "crazy" people. She clapped her hand over her mouth.

"Gee, Carla," she said. Her voice was softer and more gentle than I had ever heard it. "I guess I owe you an apology."

I looked over at her and smiled. "Thanks, Annie. But you know what would mean even more to me than having you say 'I'm sorry'?"

She shook her head.

"Letting me teach you how to read."

Quickly she stuck out her chin. "Who says I can't read?"

Now it was my turn to speak in a really soft, gentle voice. "Oh, Annie, it's nothing to be ashamed of. You're hardly alone. Besides, it's not whether or not you can read that matters. It's whether or not you recognize how important reading is—and whether or not you're ready to make a commitment to learning."

"Oh, yeah?" Her words were tough, but a lot of the bite had gone out of her tone. "And who's going to teach me?"

"I am. That is, if you'll let me."

Annie's eyes narrowed. "Wait a minute. You mean you're willing to give up a whole bunch of your time to sit with me and teach me how to read? You would really do that?"

I nodded.

"Why? Why would you want to bother?"

"Because I know how wonderful reading is, Annie. I've had books take me to the South Seas and to the moon and to little towns just like the one where we live. And I've met wonderful people in books, people I'll think of as friends for the rest of my life." I held up the diary. "Without being able to read, I never would have met Charlotte. And I want to share all that with you."

"Because you feel sorry for me?"

"Because I *like* you, Annie. And because I'd really like to be your friend. If you'll let me, that is."

Annie thought for a minute. "Homemade ice cream, huh? I wonder what flavors they had back then."

"Strawberry, maybe. Vanilla. And I certainly hope they had chocolate!"

"Probably no rocky road, though." Annie was grinning. "That's my favorite."

"You know, I bet if we read through Charlotte's diary together, we can find out exactly what flavors people used to eat back then."

"Maybe . . . maybe I could even find out by myself." Sounding a little bit breathless, she added, "After you teach me how to read, I mean."

I just looked at her and smiled. "Annie, that sounds like a great idea."

chapter
ten

"So how did it go?" Betsy asked for the thirteenth time as I strode down Greenlawn Street, toward the tumbledown gray church.

She and Samantha were a few paces behind, barely able to keep up with me. I was practically flying. In fact, given the way I was feeling, I'm surprised I wasn't actually walking a few inches above the ground. And it wasn't only the possibility that we were about to solve the mystery and discover what the treasure was, either; it was also knowing that I had finally gotten through to Annie.

And I intended to tell Betsy and Sam all about it, the very first chance I got. At the moment, however, I had other things on my mind.

"I'll tell you all about it as soon as we've found the treasure," I insisted. "I promise."

As we neared the site of the old church, I remembered that the other time the Bubble Gum Gang had gone snooping around in search of buried treasure, the day had been rainy, cold, and gray. This time, it was nippy, but sunny and bright. Even so, once we stopped at the edge of the churchyard, it suddenly felt a little bit colder and a whole lot gloomier. We just stood there for a minute or two, staring.

The churchyard had looked small from the sidewalk, but now that I was looking at it more carefully, I could see that it stretched pretty far back. All of it was overgrown with weeds, though, some of them waist-high. The trees, with their black bark, looked craggy. Their trunks were covered with gnarly vines. I could make out a winding path that led from the sidewalk into the thick growth, but after only a few feet it was covered up by stubby dark green growth.

The church itself loomed not far beyond. It was in terrible condition; the roof was completely caved in on one side. The stained-glass windows that Charlotte's grandmother had written about in her poem were long gone. In fact, there were hardly any windows left at all. The building reminded me of a sagging, gray face with big empty eyes staring out. When I shivered, it had little to do with the frosty November wind.

"Gee," Samantha finally said in a strange voice. "I never noticed before how creepy this place looks."

"Me, either," said Betsy. "You might even say it's kind of spooky." She was clutching one of the rotting pickets on the fence that surrounded the churchyard. I noticed it was crumbling in her hand.

"Oh, the spookiest thing we'll encounter will probably be a few spiders," I remarked with forced cheerfulness. "And they'll probably be a lot more scared of us than we are of them."

I looked over at the two of them. "All set?"

Samantha and Betsy looked at each other, swallowing hard. For a minute there, I was afraid they were going to change their minds. But then I reminded myself that the Bubble Gum Gang always comes through. And this time was no exception.

"Let's go," Samantha said. She actually managed to sound enthusiastic.

When we pushed open the front gate, more of the fence came off in our hands. I looked at the chunk I ended up holding, not knowing what to make of it.

"Shopping for souvenirs?" Betsy joked. I burst out laughing. Suddenly, none of this seemed quite so scary anymore.

"Come on, you two. We're in for a real adventure," I said. Now filled with confidence, I led the way.

As we tromped through the overgrown weeds, I recited the poem. " '. . . Go where voices sing a gentle song, where faces lift toward heaven, where sunlight streams through colored glass . . .' "

"It's hard to believe this place ever looked like that," Samantha commented.

"If you use your imagination, and squint a

little . . ." Betsy paused to try it out. After a few seconds she shook her head. "Nope. Can't picture it."

"That's okay," I said. "It's being able to follow the clues that counts."

"Here's the front door," Betsy said not long after. "I guess we have to go around to the back."

"Spiders, here we come," said Samantha. I noticed she pulled her thick fuzzy mittens up a little further.

We had to step over some huge branches that had fallen off the trees—probably during past thunderstorms, I decided. I realized that no one had been in here to clean up for a really long time. Years, probably. Even decades. Somehow, knowing we were the first ones to come through here in a very long time made the whole thing feel even eerier.

"Here's the back," I said heartily. I turned around, scanning the churchyard. Suddenly I got a funny feeling in my stomach. I could see where this was leading.

Betsy and Samantha were still a step behind me.

"Okay," said Betsy, looking around. "We have to find something that there's seven of. 'Behind, at number seven . . .' See anything that sounds like that?"

"I do," said Samantha. "Look at those trees. There are seven of them, all lined up in a row. See? One, two, three, four, five . . ."

"Do they lead to some stones?" Betsy held her hand up over her eyes, to form a visor, so she could gaze across the churchyard. Finally, she saw what I had seen. "Oh, no."

"Not another parking lot?" Samantha cried.

"Worse," I said. "Look what's back there."

"A cemetery," Betsy breathed. "An old cemetery."

"So that's what the 'stones' are," said Samantha. "They're gravestones."

"Right." Betsy's voice was almost a whisper. "The 'stones that last and last.' "

I gulped. "Let's go down and poke around. "We'll have to find 'the oldest on the hill.' " I checked their faces. "Are you two coming with me?"

They hesitated.

"Come on!" I pleaded. "We're almost there."

Still they stood still.

"Buried treasure!" I reminded them. "Think of it!"

No movement.

"Well, I'm going, with or without you."

Alarmed, Samantha glanced at Betsy. "We can't let her go alone! She could get lost, or trip on the weeds, or . . . or . . ."

"Or get chased by a ghost?" Betsy added.

I nearly jumped out of my skin before I realized she was only joking. "Come on, you brave treasure hunters. Let's go check this out."

We were laughing as we counted the trees up to number seven and then started examining the gravestones, searching for the oldest one. Even so, this whole thing felt really creepy. Everything was so quiet. Nothing had been disturbed for what seemed like ages. And now that Betsy had mentioned ghosts, I kept glancing over my shoulder, startled by every little noise I heard.

Still, it wasn't long before we got so caught up in our mission that we forgot all about being scared.

"Hey, look at this gravestone!" Samantha cried. "It's dated 1773!"

"That's nothing," Betsy countered. "Here's one from 1723!"

A lot of them were very old, I noted. What a fascinating place! As I read each gravestone, I found myself wondering about the person it was meant to memorialize. All these people who had at one time lived in Hanover, just like me. Just like Charlotte. I realized that I, too, was part of history, just as they were. And they all mattered just as much as I did, each and every one of them. Having walked through here, having lived in this place, was something we all had in common, something we shared. I took a moment to thank Charlotte for teaching me that.

And then, suddenly, Betsy let out a yelp.

"Hey, look over here! I think I found the oldest on the hill!"

I glanced up and saw she had moved past the cemetery, to what looked like nothing more than another clump of very high weeds. Yet when she reached over and parted them, I saw there was a gravestone back there, nearly hidden by the overgrowth.

"It's dated 1699!" she cried. "It says 'To Ebenezer Thomas Hanover, Our Beloved Father.' "

"He must have been the founder of this town!" Samantha cried.

"Gee, you never know who you'll meet in a cemetery," I commented.

But I wasn't in the mood for a history lesson. I had more important things on my mind—like buried treasure.

I hurried over to that spot, glanced at the gravestone, and then figured out which way was east. I was nervous as I looked over in that direction, hoping against hope I'd find a valley there.

Sure enough; there was a valley. No parking lot, no housing development, just a big open field that drooped in the middle. Enough of a valley for me.

"There it is!" I cried, pointing. "The valley! We're almost there!"

It was a matter of seconds before Betsy and Samantha were at my side, the three of us carefully measuring out small steps. Facing east, going deeper and deeper into the small valley, we each watched our feet as we counted.

"Twenty-five, twenty-six, twenty-seven," I breathed. My heart was pounding away, about a mile a minute. About *ten* miles a minute. I was mere inches away from the buried treasure. "Twenty-eight . . . twenty-nine!"

I stopped. I looked. I saw nothing but a small

pond—and more weeds, of course. The pounding of my heart stopped.

"Now what?" I cried. "Are we supposed to start digging?"

"I never thought to bring a shovel," Samantha said. "Wait a second. Let me see that poem."

Dutifully I handed it over to Betsy. She read it, frowning. "It doesn't say anything about the treasure being buried," she finally said. "In fact, from the way this is worded, I'd say the treasure should be right here, staring us in the face."

By now my heart had all but given up. It just kind of sat there in my chest, taking up space and weighing a whole lot more than it had ever weighed before.

"Let me see that." It was Samantha's turn to check the poem. " 'Count twenty-nine,' " she read aloud, " 'and there you'll find the treasure.' Betsy's right. It does sound like it should be right here."

"But I don't see anything!" I wailed. "Just this stupid old pond!"

Betsy and Samantha exchanged looks of sympathy.

"I never really thought the treasure would still be here," Samantha said gently. "Not after all the time that's gone by."

"But we still had the thrill of the treasure hunt," Betsy pointed out. "And you have to admit, it *was* fun."

"But now it's over," said Sam. "Hey, I know. Why don't we all go over to YoYo's to celebrate the successful treasure hunt? Maybe we didn't find the actual treasure, but we managed to follow the clues up to the end."

Betsy nodded. "That's a great idea! And Carla can tell us all about Annie and how she's about to change her life. That's what really matters, you know, not finding some treasure that somebody wrote a poem about a hundred years ago."

"I'll race you out of here!" Samantha cried. "On your mark, get set . . ."

"Go ahead," I muttered, without looking at them. "I'll be up in a couple of minutes."

Another look passed between them. "Sure, Carla. Come on, Betsy. Let's race."

When they were gone, I sank to the ground, sitting down on a big rock that happened to be there at the edge of the little pond. I was so disappointed, I felt like crying. I had put so much hope into this treasure hunt! I had wanted so badly to believe that the treasure was still here! Now, I'd never be able to solve the mystery. I'd never know what the treasure was. The thing that mattered more to Charlotte's grandmother than anything on earth. The thing she loved the most, that had the greatest worth . . .

I leaned forward, wanting to pull out a blade of grass, something to toy with as I sat there, just thinking and feeling sorry for myself. As I did, I suddenly caught sight of something that made me jump.

My reflection. Leaning over the smooth water of

the pond on such a bright and sunny day, I could see my own face perfectly.

I sat there, staring, for what seemed a long, long time. Slowly, it was all clicking into place.

The treasure. *I* was the treasure.

And eighty years earlier, Charlotte's grandmother had concocted this treasure hunt to show her the exact same thing: that *she* was a treasure. To her grandmother, she was what mattered more than anything on earth. She was the treasure she most loved, the one with the greatest worth. And she had wanted Charlotte to realize that. Skinny or not, a social outcast or not, she mattered to the people who loved her.

Finally I understood. To the people who cared about me, I, too, was a treasure. People like my parents and my sister. And my friends, Samantha and Betsy.

And Annie Cooper.

I sat there a while longer. But now, there were tears in my eyes. But not tears of sadness, not by any means. No, these were tears of gratitude.

"Thank you, Charlotte," I whispered. "And thanks to your grandmother, too."

"Are you coming?" I heard Betsy call down to me. The sound of her voice made me jump. For a while, I had forgotten all about the present.

But now, suddenly, I was back. And I wanted very much to be a part of it. Teaching Annie Cooper how to read, being with the best friends anybody ever had in the entire history of time . . . and being my *own* friend, stepping back and appreciating the good things about myself instead of simply agonizing over the bad.

It had been wonderful, being part of Charlotte's life. And I knew that from now on, I would feel that she was part of me. But what was even more important was that getting to know her, through her diary, made an important difference in my life. I had come to understand that I mattered. There were people who cared about me, people who loved me. In turn, I cared about them, too. And that was the best "treasure" anybody could ever hope for.

"Yes, I'm coming!" I called back, scrambling to my feet.

"Good thing!" Betsy replied. I could see her standing a few hundred yards away, grinning. "Because it just wouldn't be fun without you!"

I darted up the hill, tucking the poem into my pocket where I could keep it safe.